THE BLACKWATER
OPERATIVE

AN
ANNA
LEDIN
NOVEL

Books by L.L. Abbott

Mystery Series

Murder At First Light
Death At Deception Bay
Murder Of Crows
The Dead Of Winter
The Night Is Darkest
Conspiracy of Blood

Spy Thriller Series

The Blackwater Operative
The Phoenix Code
Rogue
Blown

Genre Fiction

The Hotel Penn
Our Forgotten Year
The Plus One

Children, Teen & Young Adult

Carole & The Secret Queen's Scarf
Order From Karoo Bridge
Unfollowed

www.LLAbbott.com

THE BLACKWATER OPERATIVE

A SUSPENSEFUL THRILLER SERIES

L.L. ABBOTT

AN
ANNA
LEDIN
NOVEL

For Drew, Aidan & Eric

THE BLACKWATER
OPERATIVE

Loyalty is hard to find.
Trust is easy to lose.
Actions speak louder than words.

—ANY AGENT THAT HAS BEEN BETRAYED

CHAPTER 1–

Sonja's feet slipped from under her as she rounded the corner at the end of the long dark hallway, sending her body crashing into the row of steel lockers lined against the wall. Her elbow jammed into the corner of the lower hinge sending a deep searing pain that ran all the way to her shoulder and the papers flying across the freshly polished linoleum floor.

She struggled to stand, scrambling across the width of the hallway grabbing the papers as quickly as she could, knowing that if they were to be found her death was the least of her worries.

The noise from the crash would have reverberated through the vacant building letting her pursuers know she had escaped. Sonja could feel the sweat rise on the surface of her skin making it hard to hold onto the papers as she hugged them to her body in disheveled clumps. She made it past the Dean's office and stopped at the end of the hall, trying to decide which direction would be the safest for her to flee. She had to find a way to somehow hide the documents.

Each door she tried was locked and panic began to rise as she reached the end of the hall. She turned the handle on the staff room and the door flew open and she pulled herself around the door, closing quietly once she was inside. Leaving the light off, she made her way over to the counter where the envelopes were kept and dumped the crumpled pieces of paper down. She knew they were out of order, but that didn't matter.

Stiffness was beginning to build in her elbow and the sleeve of her shirt was sticking to her skin, making her aware of the blood that was pooling underneath. She just hoped that there wasn't a trail of blood on the floor outside the hall.

During her year working with Professor Abraham, she spent many hours photocopying documents for him and knew where the envelopes were stored. Once the papers were relatively flat, she reached up and grabbed a large manila envelope, and proceeded to place the pieces of paper inside. She ran to the photocopy machine and flipped the paper storage door open and extracted a plain sheet from the tray. She lay it on the counter next to the envelope and reached for a thick black marker and quickly removed the lid, fumbling as it released, and she sent it rolling across the length of the counter until it dropped to the floor. Sonja froze, hoping the sound hadn't revealed her position. Confident she hadn't been discovered, she began to scribble out her note hoping that her handwriting was legible. The combination of the darkness and the thickness of the marker made her concerned that he wouldn't be able to read the instructions. As she moved her hand from left to right across the crisp

2

white sheet, she could feel the side of her palm drag over the paper and she knew she was leaving a trail of blood on the note.

Maybe that would ensure the importance of the package. She placed the note inside the envelope and licked the seal and pressed it closed. Then, wanting to make sure that the envelope stayed sealed until it reached its final destination, she pulled a strip of tape from the tape dispenser and pressed the strip over the sealed flap.

She printed the name and address on the front and slid the envelope in the outbox, placing its fate in the hands of the secretary the next morning.

Sonja pressed her ear on the door frame and listened over the sound of her own heart pounding for any sign of movement in the hall. Once she was sure there was no noise, she released the lock on the door handle and slowly opened it. The soft glow of the emergency night lights illuminated the empty hall as she stepped out of the room, locking the door before she pulled it shut. Sonja checked one more time to make sure the door was locked, and then with the sleeve of her sweater, she wiped the handle clean of any blood. She then ran toward the exit.

The blood pumping in her head made it difficult to listen for approaching steps. Her breathing was heavy and her chest was feeling tight from the toxic fumes she inhaled from when her attacker first tried to restrain her. She let out a sigh as she caught sight of the red exit light above the steel door leading to the parking lot, and reached into the front pocket of her jeans, and pulled out her car key, she wanted to be ready.

Her hand was on the door when she heard the building pace of footsteps approaching from behind. She knew if she opened the door the sound would echo through the hall, and she wasn't sure she could make it to her car before being caught. She turned around to her left and then to her right but could see no room or hall to escape into. She eyed the row of lockers and began to pull at each one until finally one opened and she stepped inside. She was small enough to be able to turn around and face the front of the locker and pulled it shut, tugging at the air vents to make sure it was completely closed.

A few seconds later the sound of muffled footsteps grew louder until Sonja knew they were within a couple of feet from where she was hiding. Her heart pounded so hard that she was sure they would be able to hear it in the hall. She forced her breathing down to short quiet spurts and she felt like she was going to pass out. Her lungs were burning, and she had to contract her stomach to keep from coughing or gasping for air inside the stale locker.

The deep voices of two men were close enough to hear but their words were inaudible, however, she knew why they were looking for her. That's how the agency always did it, they sent two for the kill, just to make sure.

Sonja stretched her neck, so she could see through the air vents, and because of their angle, she could only see the lower part of their bodies. She saw the fresh burn on the hand of one of the attackers and let herself feel some pleasure in knowing she fought back.

They were both large and in great shape, and she knew she wouldn't have been able to outrun them. She tried to lean closer to the door to hear what they were saying but she struggled to make sense of the words. She didn't want to risk being heard so she did her best from where she was crammed and pushed along the back of the locker, hoping she wouldn't be seen. She knew enough Russian to make out that they were looking for her and the papers, but beyond that, she was at a loss.

After a while, her two attackers gave up their search and returned in the direction that they came. Sonja could hear their steps as they pounded along the hall and then the subtle shift in pace as their feet stepped closer together when they began to turn the corner. She counted to ten once the sound of their steps ceased and then she quietly pushed the locker door open and stepped out into the hall.

She made a dash for the door and leaned on the bar with both hands and released it from the frame. Without stopping or looking back, she ran in a straight line to her car. The damp night air felt cool on her skin, especially where the sweat-soaked her short brown hair. She jumped over the low-lying hedges and ran through the front flower bed, not worrying about anything except shortening the distance between her and her car.

She reached the top of the stone steps, taking them two at a time while holding the railing with her right hand, sliding most of the way to the bottom. She landed on the pavement at the base of the steps and broke into a full run.

Her rusted red Toyota was parked under the light post that was marked with an oversized letter Q. She stretched out her right hand and frantically pushed the unlock button on her remote until the lights flashed and she knew the car door was open.

Sonja jumped over the grassy knoll and landed right next to her car. She placed her left hand on the handle just as the explosive force pushed her body against the side of her car. A dizzying faintness washed through her and chills began to tingle her skin. She looked down and saw where the bullet had shattered her car window when it exited her body. Her grey sweater slowly began to absorb the dark red blood as it seeped from her body and soaked across the front of her top until the university logo was completely darkened. She fell against the car and the weight of her body pulled her down until she was resting on her knees with her face flat against the side of the door. Her hands made a squeaking noise as they slid across the metal until her body finally crumpled to the ground and she was sprawled across the pavement. The chill she felt on the surface of her skin was replaced with a wave of warmth, and then finally nothing.

She lay staring up at the night sky and watched as the stars slowly danced above. A childhood song played in her head and she knew it was time to let go. She had done what she came to do and now the rest was up to Josh. She could only hope that the papers reached him in time.

CHAPTER 2-

Anna Ledin's last day at the agency was not a day she liked to remember but it was also one she had trouble forgetting. The sound of the explosion still haunted her and she would awaken in a cold sweat in the middle of the night as her dreams morphed into nightmares and took her back to that day when one wrong decision changed her life forever.

It took her a whole year before she was able to sleep through the night without any pills, but that didn't stop the nightmares from coming. Not as often, but they still came. Tomorrow was going to mark two years since she walked away from her position as Special Investigator with the CIA. The toll the physical and emotional pain took on her after the accident was too much to overcome and she refused to let her ego allow any more innocent people to be harmed, or worse, die because of it.

Anna knew she was great at her job. At one point she was one of the best. She was top of her class at the academy and her supervisors fast-tracked her into the field because of her insanely innate ability to read terrorist threats and how they related to international economic trends, making her an invaluable profiler. She spoke five languages and none with the hint of an accent which made her perfect for undercover agent work.

She was average height, about 5'7", and wore her sandy brown hair shoulder length. She had a naturally athletic body that allowed her to easily mask her core strength within her frame without the necessity of excessive bulk. Anna's strong cardio was essential in gaining the respect of the other agents in training, because no matter how arduous the task, she could always keep up, and even exceed some of her classmates during their highly competitive drills.

Because of her professional approach to her job, she continued to gain the respect of fellow agents and supervisors in the field. Anna established a network in both allied and competing global agencies that she could draw on during any of her assignments whenever she needed to count on cooperation outside the department.

In her last year with the agency, Anna was the lead investigator on a serious threat that came in from one of her many reliable contacts when she was alerted of a possible terrorist attack during the Super Bowl Game in Chicago. The head of Homeland Security was a big football fan and an even bigger Bears fan and he insisted that the site be secured and the game not be canceled.

A toxic gas leak was supposed to be triggered by a rigged lighting system but by the time Anna had a crew of electrical experts in place, she realized the terrorist threat was a decoy for a more strategic attack. While Anna and her team were poised to be prepared for the attack at the stadium, the agency head office was the real target.

Unlike most agency offices, they weren't located in Langley. For twenty years they ran a covert operation in the safe, secure remote location that served as a hub for training and operations for one of the most elite groups of special agents the CIA had employed. Outside of the President and his executive council, no one knew about the agency's Chicago offshoot.

In the span of one afternoon, it was all brought down into a pile of rubble claiming the lives of over one hundred and fifty personnel. Agents, supervisors, support staff, tech wizards. All that was left was Anna and her team who were fighting the decoy threat. By the time Anna realized what the real target was, the phone lines had been compromised and disconnected and the only hope she had at reaching her team was to drive directly to the office to warn them. She was within a block when the explosion hit, and the thunderous shudder reverberated from the ground into the seat of her car and she knew she was too late.

The type of work the agency did was extremely demanding and Anna grew close to everyone she worked with. They were more than friends, they became family. No one had time for family life outside the agency, and eventually, you learned that having one just made you more vulnerable to your enemies. Anna lost a lot of people she cared about in that explosion. Two people were especially important to her. Her partner Denis Evans and her commander William Lewis.

Denis and Anna went through training together and learned to lean on each other for support as opposed to seeing each other as rivals. They had the same sense of humor and focus on their job, and Denis didn't see Anna's exemplary skill and strength as a weakness in himself, which some of the other male recruits often did.

Denis was 5'10" and had light brown hair and deep green eyes. His broad shoulders extended beyond his waist by a few inches and the superb strength that he had amazed Anna each time they worked out together. Anna fought her attraction to him believing that it was more valuable to have him as a partner at work than in life. After the explosion, Anna wasn't sure that was the right decision, and each time she glanced at the tattoo on her wrist that matched the one Denis had on his, she was flooded with grief.

Commander Lewis was her boss and the last connection she had to her father, and he was possibly the person she was closest to in her life. William was responsible for Anna's training when began, and although he saw an incredible talent in the young rising star, he tried his best to discourage her from joining the agency. He worked her harder than the other recruits and made her run through drills intended for veterans instead of students. In the end, Anna had excelled beyond what even William thought she could, and he could no longer deny her a position in the agency. He did insist, however, that she be on his team.

William treated Anna like a daughter and ever since her father died, he took the extra responsibility of guiding her and protecting her throughout her life. William felt responsible for Anna's father's death and he told her he would spend his whole life making up for what she had lost.

Commander Lewis stood more than six feet tall and his imposing stature commanded the attention of everyone in the room when he spoke. William had two Ivy League college degrees and was a respected leader in the same black community he was raised in. He was always Commander Lewis at work, but at home, he was Uncle Will.

The swipe card records showed they were both in the building when the explosion ripped through the four floors of concrete and steel, leaving no possible chance that anyone could have escaped.

After that, Anna could no longer trust her instinct and skill in the field. If she could let the two most important people in her life die, how could she trust she wouldn't let anyone else down. The date of the explosion was tattooed on the inside of her left wrist and each day it reminded her to never forget Denis or William.

Anna eventually settled into a position as a social worker with an inner-city office, using a connection to get the job that could help her disappear. At least she knew she would be spending her efforts helping people and not harming them.

Today was the second Tuesday of the month which meant that she was having her regular meeting with Devon. He was eighteen now but was orphaned at fifteen and it took every ounce of Anna's fight to get Devon placed in a secure environment away from the pull of the street gangs. She wanted to make sure he had a fair chance in life and education was the best place to start. She couldn't bring back his parents, but she could try her best to give him a leg up in the world.

Anna pulled a thick cable knit sweater over her head and tugged on the hem pulling it below the waistline on her jeans. It was one her mother knit for her when she first took up skiing, and no matter how many times she put it on she felt the same close feeling to her mother when she wore it. She slung her bag diagonally across her chest and grabbed her keys from the kitchen counter.

She bounded down the four flights of her building and exited on the street to face the regular morning mass of bodies making their way toward the subway station. She glanced at her watch and saw that she had just enough time to pick up a couple of bagels from Devon's favorite deli. Anna picked up her pace and slipped into line at Dean's Deli and waved to the owner who was waiting on the customer directly in front of her. When it was her turn, she stepped up and greeted Dean with a wide smile.

"Good morning, Dean," Anna said. "I'm going to need two of your cinnamon raisin bagels and one tall coffee."

"I have them right here for you," Dean reached over to the counter behind where he was standing and grabbed the brown paper bag, and handed it to Anna.

"Let me just get your coffee," Dean proceeded to fill the travel mug with the perfect mix of coffee and cream that Anna grew accustomed to.

"Today is your day with Devon isn't it?" Dean asked.

"Yes, it is," Anna answered. "He graduates this spring and I am helping him fill out college applications."

"Wish him luck for me," Dean said.

Anna reached into her pocket and handed Dean a twenty-dollar bill.

He pulled back his hand and shook his head and said, "It's on me today. A gift for Devon."

Anna thanked him and scurried past the other customers that were waiting in line, narrowly missing the man who was standing directly behind her.

She ran the rest of the way to the subway station and pushed through the gates slipping a token into the slot releasing the turnstile from its locked position. The train was emerging from the damp tunnel and she smiled at the perfect timing she coordinated today, coffee and bagels in tow.

The train screeched as it neared the platform where a horde of commuters was awaiting its impending arrival. Instinctively Anna moved back a step as the train entered the station, letting the previous passengers exit the car before stepping inside and making her way to the back row. Anna still couldn't shake all her training and always liked being able to see everyone on the train.

As the doors closed and the train began to pull away from the station, she leaned her head against the back of the seat and looked out the window. Soon the train would surface, and she enjoyed getting lost in the movement of the train as it snaked its way through the city toward her office downtown.

Anna watched a young child seated a few rows in front of her as he bounced with seemingly endless energy as his mother did her best to keep his foot from hitting the man sitting opposite of them.

The sensation of being watched was a familiar feeling from the times she was on assignment. But she wasn't on assignment, she was on her way to meet Devon.

Still not able to shake the feeling, and only moving her eyes, she shifted them slightly toward the figure standing on the left side of the train car and saw that a man was staring directly at her. He quickly averted his eyes toward a paper he was holding, and she told herself that she was just being paranoid. As the car approached the next station, she rose from her seat and maneuvered her way through the standing passengers, and waited by the door. She stood to wait with her right arm clasped to the handrail, watching the rooftops pass by as the train began to descend into the station tunnel.

As soon as the car entered the darkened tunnel the outside view changed, and the bright blue sky was replaced with reflections of the other passengers that, like Anna, waited for the train to reach the station. As she continued to look straight ahead, she caught the reflection of the man who was watching her in the glass of the door. He was standing behind her, only separated by a few passengers. As the doors pulled apart the clump of bodies began their unified exit to the street.

Anna quickened her pace and caught a reflection of the same man following her in the electrical box, as she swerved through the crowd. She reached the stairs and bounded up, two at a time until she reached the top of the stairs. The security mirror reflected the passengers climbing the stairs, and she saw him push by a group as he tried to catch up to her.

14

Anna dumped her coffee cup into the garbage can as she passed the ticket booth and pushed through the crowd of commuters and slipped out the door. She began to walk east keeping her body as close to the storefronts as she could. After a few minutes, she glanced over her left shoulder and saw the grey slacks and black loafers that the man was wearing scurrying through the morning crowds and heading in her direction.

A grocer was arguing with a man in front of his shop and she decided to take advantage of the distraction and run into his store and exit into the back lane. Once she emerged from the store, she made a quick right and ducked into a wide doorway next to the green garbage dumpster, and pushed her body back as far as she could to hide from view. If she was being followed, she counted on the man not being far behind.

She purposely made sure that he could see her running into the store from the street making it look like she was trying to lose him. The familiar rush of adrenaline that she had not experienced since her time in the field was fresh, and she realized how much she missed that feeling.

Soon she heard the shuffling sound of the black loafers landing on the broken, gravel-covered pavement of the back lane. And she silently counted 3 . . .2 . . .1.

Just as the man came into her line of sight, Anna reached out with her right hand and grabbed hold of his wrist, twisting as she pulled it up toward the back of his neck, while she simultaneously landed her left hand on his opposite shoulder swinging his body until he faced the brick wall of the building. He squeezed his shoulder blades together as she pushed his wrist closer to the base of his neck and slammed the weight of his body into the side of the building. He began to writhe under her grip, and she slammed her knee into the base of his back hitting that exact nerve point that rendered his lower body immobile. A move she learned from Aki Nakamura when she was training in Japan and had employed on many similar occasions.

"Why are you following me?" Anna leaned in close to the back of his head.

The man twisted and then groaned in pain. She pulled his wrist up and he screamed in agony.

"Tell me why you are following me?" Anna asked again.

The man suddenly pushed away from the wall releasing Anna's grip on his left shoulder. He brought his elbow up and jabbed it back toward Anna's face and she ducked just as it swung over the top of her head. She then pivoted on her feet and brought her right leg around with full force and landed a kick on his left ribcage, feeling the bones give away to the pressure under her foot and he howled in pain. As he bent sideways and grabbed hold of his cracked ribs, she swung her leg in the other direction and contacted the back of his knees, sending him down to the ground with a thud.

"I am going to ask you only one more time. Why are you following me?" Anna was positioned directly over the man, blocking his escape.

"Because I sent him," the words came from behind her. She turned in the direction of the voice, and as she faced him her brow crumpled in confusion and she yelled.

"You're supposed to be dead!"

CHAPTER 3-

"You haven't lost your touch, I see," William nodded his head toward the man who was now sprawled face down, incapacitated on the ground next to them.

"He'll be okay," Anna said, "Just a few cracked ribs."

"And maybe a bruised ego," William added.

Anna stood in shock as she took in the familiar features that were imprinted into her memory, especially his warm, dark eyes which were what she remembered most about him. Her eyes then darted to the left side of his face and to the massive scar left by a burn.

William pulled back the collar of his shirt and tilted his head, "A little reminder of two years ago," once Anna got a clear view of his skin, he let the collar snap back into place.

"I ... I ...," Anna tried to fight the tears that she worked so hard to suppress. "I thought you were dead."

"I was," William responded. "Or at least everyone had to think I was."

"I know, but that's for everyone else. We're like family. Damn it, William. We are family!" Anna lunged forward and threw her arms around William's neck. She sobbed into his jacket and he put his arms around her and held her tight. Just like he did the day she found out her father had died.

"I'm sorry Anna. I wanted to contact you sooner, but, I couldn't." William began to explain.

"Why?" Anna pulled back and faced William as she wiped the tears with the back of her hand.

"It was for your own safety," William said. "Look, let's get Joe up off the ground and I'll explain everything to you."

They guided the injured agent to a car that was waiting at the end of the lane, and Anna thought about apologizing for breaking his ribs, but then remembered it wasn't the way she was trained. She knew Joe learned a valuable lesson today, and she was the one who delivered it. Once they were relieved of Joe and his injuries, Anna and William made their way to another waiting vehicle and crawled up into the back of the blacked-out SUV.

"I need to ask you, William," Anna began. "What about Denis?"

"I'm sorry Anna, he died in the explosion. His office was next to mine and the explosion went off just as he passed by my door and said good morning."

William tilted his head back and looked at the roof of the SUV. He knew it was only a matter of time before he had to explain the explosion to Anna, he just wasn't looking forward to it.

"You know by now that we were compromised and that we were the intended target. With our resources and focus elsewhere, we left ourselves open to distraction at our home base," William shook his head.

"You have no idea how many times I replay that day trying to remember if there was a sign that I missed. Could I've avoided the whole attack?" Tears lined the bottom rim of William's eyes. "So many good people died that day, and I'm ultimately responsible."

"We all were William," Anna said. "I still have nightmares about that day. I should've seen the discrepancies in the intel. I looked over the file for months after that day and I still couldn't see the hole."

"That's because there was none," William said.

"I came to the same conclusion as well. And as much as I hate to admit it, if I had to make the call again, I probably would. There was no sign that we were the intended target."

"The explosion came with no warning and caught everyone off guard. Susan was fixing a jam in the photocopier, Chris was just back from the field and catching up on his report, and Denis was late getting in and had stopped by my office to say good morning. It was just a typical boring day. Then without a warning, there was a thundering sound and the floor began to shift below us. I can still remember the roof folding in on top of me in my office. I dove under my desk just as the floor collapsed. The whole building crumbled and I was the only one who survived," William paused before continuing. "I must've been knocked unconscious because all I can remember is the sound of sirens. There was dust everywhere from the explosion and I managed to make it to cover of the trees and stayed hidden near the river."

"I was a block away when I heard the explosion," Anna recalled.

"I know. I saw you drive up and the emergency personnel had to pull you away. You were trying to get into the building," William remembered that day like it was yesterday. The sound of Anna's screams was as real today as they were two years ago.

"Why didn't you call out to me?" Anna asked.

"You know the protocol we devised if we thought we were compromised," William explained.

Anna nodded, knowing she would've done the same thing.

"Anyways, I went to a safehouse I had in Canada and laid low for a while. I dug around for a bit and I didn't like what I was hearing or reading," William explained.

"About what?" Anna asked.

"It was an inside job, Anna. The threat was set up to look like it was a terrorist attack, but it was closer than that," William handed Anna a file and she flipped it open and began to read the information that William had collected over the last two years.

"Are you sure about this?" Anna regretted the question as it left her lips.

"I didn't want to believe it either, but I can assure you that it's true," William nodded toward the file. "You can see I've spent a lot of time on this."

"Why?" Anna closed the file.

"Someone has infiltrated the government and there seems to be a plot involving several resource companies that leaves them vulnerable to take-overs from foreign nationals. It could be China or Russia, we're not sure. There's a faction in our government working to manipulate tariffs and exports intended to weaken regulations and controlling the flow of specific goods."

"Then why not just expose them?" Anna asked, "Why did you stay hidden all this time? You know enough people that you could have gone to for help."

"Who knew about us Anna?" William asked.

"Just the President and his executive council," Anna answered.

"We don't know where the leak was, and we have to assume it is pretty high up," William paused. "That's why I remained in hiding, and that's why I'm here now."

"You think I know who the leak was?" Anna asked.

"No, but you can help find out," William said. "I've done everything I can, but as you can see with Joe's performance, I haven't been able to put together a decent team."

"He may be better suited to behind the scenes work," Anna suggested.

"That's why I need you, Anna," William pleaded.

"No," Anna handed the file back to William. "I don't trust my instincts anymore."

William put his hand over hers, "But I do. I trust you with my life."

Anna just looked back at him, not able to speak.

"Look, I'm not going to sugar coat this, but I need someone with your skill, your connections and because you have been out for a couple of years, you can just jump right in and not be suspected."

"I don't know William," the hesitation was obvious in Anna's voice.

"It is more than just a request, Anna. We can't do this without you." William wasn't going to let Anna leave without having her onboard.

Anna just smiled and shook her head knowing she had lost the battle.

"Good. Now let's get those cinnamon bagels to Devon and then you can let your boss know you're quitting."

CHAPTER 4-

Anna wasn't surprised to find out that William was behind Devon's acceptance to Howard University. He knew the best way to get Anna to agree to leave everything behind was to help her take care of Devon, and then she could devote her full attention to William's new covert task force.

Once Devon was settled, Anna let her supervisor know it was time to move on and even though her supervisor was disappointed, she didn't question her decision. Everyone at the office knew that Anna was overqualified for the job she was doing, and her supervisor always suspected that Anna was forcing the boredom on herself as a means of an escape.

Anna had committed to being part of William's team, but she had a few conditions. She was intent on working alone, and all documentation was to be as restrictive as they could make it, and they coordinated a drop place for information.

It was ten o'clock and Anna was almost finished setting a surveillance system in her apartment. Her connection with Alastair was her most valuable connection when she was in the field.

Alastair Sewell was the technology guru at MI6 for the last fifteen years. His mind worked in ways that the typical agents didn't. He was responsible for outfitting agents with such intricate devices that he left his own superiors wondering how he could create spy gadgets that were so removed from reality. He hadn't dreamed of a career with MI6 or any government agency for that matter. It was quite the opposite.

When British Intelligence became aware of Alastair, it was because they were being attacked by him. His misguided youth and advanced technological intellect paired with his imagination and free time, lead him to conjure a plan to demonstrate that the British government was leaving themselves open to attack. He convinced himself that he was doing it for the safety of the British population.

However, after a couple of years of tampering with British Intelligence, Alastair was eventually caught. The head of MI6, Rupert Davies, took a keen interest in Alastair, or more specifically, his talents, and because Alastair was not a hardened criminal, Rupert offered him a job. The government's threat of a life behind bars, and the promise to make things (in Alastair's words) 'utter, bloody hell' for his mother, convinced him to agree.

If pushed, Alastair would have to admit that he enjoyed his work. He essentially could create and invent any device his imagination could dream up, and consequently, he flourished.

Anna met Alastair when their two countries joined forces on her first mission when they were tracking a terrorist plot from the Middle East that had targeted African relief agencies. In addition to working well together, they also became fast friends. Alastair was on a plane and by Anna's side after the explosion and helped her through the funerals for her coworkers.

Today Anna thought of Alastair as she placed the miniature electronic devices around her apartment. They detected and recorded movement within a ten-foot radius of where they were placed. They were the size of a seed and adhered to any surface. A key design feature was the coating that made them completely undetectable to search mechanisms. Alastair refused to share the formula with the head of MI6, making sure he always had the upper hand.

Anna had placed the final device in the corner of the ceiling in her front hall near her door. Once she had double-checked her bag, she synced her phone with the devices and left the apartment. She lived on the top floor of a four-story walk-up and the stairwell was open to the foyer below. She bounded down the stairs until she reached the landing on the ground floor. She pushed open the front door and felt a rush of cool air hit her face. She tightened the scarf around her neck and took a deep breath. She began to feel a vigor that she hadn't felt in many years. Her grief over Denis's death was still raw, however, William being alive was what she decided to draw her energy from. Now her purpose was to find out who was responsible for Denis's death and to make them pay.

Anna walked the three blocks to the library and reached the building just as a faded yellow school bus crept to a parked position in front of the building. The doors squeaked open and a frazzled teacher stepped onto the sidewalk, clipboard in hand.

"Okay class line up behind me and no pushing!" he yelled at the throng of eight-year old's that began to pour out of the bus.

Anna weaved her way around the bodies and made her way up the steps. She grabbed hold of the brass handle and pulled the over-sized wooden doors open and ducked her body inside. She loved coming to this building and was happy that the city decided to save the structure as opposed to demolishing it in favor of a modern design. She loved the way the smell of the books and the wood of the shelves enveloped her when she walked into the main library.

The book she was looking for was in the section where the classics were shelved. She reached up and pulled down the copy of Anna Karenina and flipped to page 792 and read the sequence of letters and numbers that were written in reverse order in chalk along the inside margin. Once she memorized them, she wiped the chalk from the page and replaced the book.

The coded numbers referenced another library call number, and she searched until she found the book she was looking for. Anna removed the book and made her way to the back of the stacks and found a corner on the floor that was out of the way of the eye of the librarian and security camera.

Anna opened the book and folded the hardcovers back until they touched. She peered inside the spine and reached in and removed the drive that was carefully taped on the inside. She closed the book and put it on the pile of books next to her on the floor.

She pushed the button in the middle of the jump drive and a connector extended out the end. It was a device only designed to fit into her specially equipped phone so there was no danger of someone finding it and plugging it into their laptop. She attached the connector to her phone and she used her fingerprint and password to access the file. Alastair was always aware that most people used one finger for prints, and often it was the thumb. He designed the security for the unit to require two separate fingers simultaneously to be used on the rectangular pad and if they should not register the device would be erased by the phone rendering it useless should it fall into the wrong hands.

All agents knew that if they were to give up a device and be coerced into opening it with a print, they would be dead the instant after it was unlocked. This allowed the agent to intentionally use the wrong fingerprint sequence, erasing the data. Either way, the agent was good as dead, may as well go down a hero.

She pressed her index and ring finger on the pad and after a couple of seconds, a keypad appeared on the screen and Anna keyed in the seven-digit code that she found written in Tolstoy's book and unlocked the contents of the drive.

Three files flashed up on the screen and Anna pressed the image indicated for case notes that William assembled for Anna to read. The written report was a little longer than the one William showed Anna in the back of the SUV but essentially held the same information.

There were eight attacks in total that William and his team were able to connect during his black-on-black operation. Throughout two years, there were attacks on transport trucks, a power plant, a specialized metal fabrication plant, and a water facility. The only thing any of these events had in common was that a call was made to an emergency number before the attack.

Each call was traced to a disposable phone and each cell number was different. However, William was able to figure out that the phones were all purchased at kiosks in various airports. Once he was able to get the security camera films for each location, he realized that the same man purchased each of the phones. The facial recognition software that their team had in place worked off the various film angles and came up with the name of one man, Logan James. He was an agent at the CIA office in Langley and worked in the Special Activities Division. What was an agent that was associated with the SAD doing mixed up in these attacks? Anna read to the end of the file and made note of Logan's address and private cell number. She closed the file and read the last remaining two documents. One was a compilation of banking information and the other copies of travel itineraries that Logan had over the last number of years.

His travel took him through the same airports where he purchased the various cell phones and since each was a connection flight on official business flights, he was never flagged. Several flights took him to Riga regularly, and in total, he racked up twelve visits over three years.

The banking information was recorded in the last file and there were various entries from three minor banks in Latvia. William must have worked on these for a while because when Anna tapped the file icon an elaborate diagram appeared on her screen and even though she knew the source was reliable, it was even hard for her to believe. Money was being deposited into various smaller banks from one large Russian corporation. Each account funneled money around to accounts within those banks until payments were made to offshore accounts whose ownership was cloaked.

Anna would've seen the link of the accounts as a stretch until she realized William indicated the final transfers from the various bank accounts all took place on the same days that Logan had traveled to Riga. Anna lowered her phone to her lap and rested her head back. There still wasn't a lot of information to go on, and the only lead she could follow was that of CIA agent Logan James.

And that was where she was going to start. She hit the sequence of keys that erased the file and burned the connections on the inside of the drive, and she waited for the green light to indicate the drive was dead.

"What is that?" A wandering eight-year-old from the school trip appeared from behind the book stack just as Anna was removing the drive from her phone.

"What? This?" Anna pulled out the drive and held it up in front of her face.

"Yeah, is it a game? You're not supposed to have a game in here!" Anna wasn't sure how loud an eight-year-old was supposed to be, but she was sure this kid was louder.

Anna whispered, trying to remember what would've piqued her attention at that age, "No, it's not a game. It's top secret."

"Like spy stuff?" the kid asked.

"Yeah, like that," Anna got up and slipped the drive in the young kid's hand and put her finger to her lip. "Don't tell anyone."

The kid's eyes sprang open, "Even my grumpy teacher?"

"Especially your grumpy teacher," Anna smiled. "Keep this safe, okay?"

The kid shoved it into his front pocket and smiled.

Anna picked up the books on the floor and began to walk toward the exit. She needed to go home and pack up some essentials. She needed to make a trip to Virginia.

CHAPTER 5-

The next morning Anna was waiting outside the building that Logan James lived in with his girlfriend and their two cats. It was a three-story brownstone that was situated within walking distance to the Special Activities Division office. It was conveniently positioned across from a small park, and Anna found a secluded bench that she could sit on unnoticed as she waited for Logan to appear from the building. All of William's intel had been accurate so far.

Right on schedule, the front doors of his building swung open and Logan and his girlfriend walked down the front steps. He turned and kissed her goodbye and then he began to walk east toward the office as she headed west toward the hospital where she worked. Anna rose from her seat on the bench and walked a safe distance behind Logan, so she could follow him and not be seen. He was the only lead she had right now, and she didn't want to blow it.

Just as William had indicated in his report, Logan stopped at the corner coffee shop and ordered a coffee and breakfast sandwich, and picked the corner booth in the back. Anna

31

realized from reading William's file that Logan was a creature of habit as most agents were. It was what helped most of them compartmentalize their private lives from their work lives.

Logan reached into his pocket and pulled out his phone and was scanning through it as he finished eating. Once he was done, he grabbed his plate, and after placing it on the counter and waved to the clerk. He walked out of the shop and down the street the remainder of the distance to his office without turning around.

Anna waited as he entered the building that housed the Special Activities Division that Logan worked in. Anna watched as he extracted the phone from his pocket and held it against the scanner pad and entered through an unmanned door to the side of the building. She continued to watch Logan until the door closed behind him and she heard the thud of the steel door as it closed, hoping it indicated that he was in for the remainder of the day.

Anna walked the mile back to his apartment and turned the corner a few feet from the building and made her way to the back lane. She walked until she recognized the backside of the brownstone and she scanned the area to make sure nobody was watching.

She took her lockpick out of her pocket and within ten seconds had released the two separate locks on the service door of the building. Once inside, it wasn't the type of building that had security guards and Anna made her way up the stairwell without being noticed or questioned.

She slipped the lockpick into both the handle and deadlock on Logan's apartment and was amused at the ease at which she entered his home. She was prepared for more difficulty entering the home of a CIA agent and thought of the devices that she set up around her apartment before she left.

It didn't take Anna long to walk around the apartment to get a feel for how Logan lived. It was 850 square feet so that made it easy to determine how Logan went about his daily routine. Anna found what she was looking for on the kitchen counter. Next to the blender, there was a charging cord still plugged into the outlet on the wall. Anna worked quickly to remove the plate over the outlet and unscrew the wires from the back of the electrical plugs.

One of the cats jumped up onto the counter and began to rub up against her arm as she quickly removed the wires. She gently pushed the cat and it gave her a meow as it walked to the other end of the counter and then plopped its oversized body down.

She reached into her bag and pulled out a matching electrical unit and attached the power wires to it. Once it was connected, she pressed the button on the back to activate the internal cloning device software. She rubbed her eyes that had begun to water because of the cat and she tried to hurry as she finished the connection. She pushed it back into place in the wall and replaced the receptacle plate and plugged the power chord back into the outlet.

Next, she needed to search the bedroom and scanned the room until she found the exercise tracker that he left on the night table. She picked it up, flipped it over, and attached the exercise tracker to her phone. Within a few seconds, all of Logan's information was uploaded to her system and she was able to install a tracking code back onto his unit, so she could follow him when he was wearing it.

She replaced it in the same position on the night table and started to leave when she heard a key in the lock. She dropped to the floor and crawled under the bed and wiggled her way to the center.

She could hear Logan's girlfriend rummaging around in the kitchen for something as she spoke to the cat in a high-pitched voice as it continued to lay sprawled out on the counter.

"Where did I put my pass?" Anna could hear the kitchen drawers open and slam closed.

She then could hear footsteps making their way around the living room and then into the bedroom. One of the cats ran ahead of Logan's girlfriend trying to stay out of the way and dashed under the bed and slid to a stop when it came face to face with Anna. The cat began to hiss at Anna's intrusion into its private hiding place. Thankfully Logan's girlfriend didn't notice.

Anna continued to watch from under the bed as she walked around the room to her night table where she opened the top drawer, all the while keeping a close eye on the hissing cat. As she was digging around in the drawer for her pass, she knocked over a book and it fell on the floor near the edge of the bed. Anna closed her eyes and tried her best to not sneeze.

"Here it is!" she shouted.

Finally, Anna thought, knowing it was only a matter of time before she would sneeze, or that the cat would reveal her presence.

She watched as Logan's girlfriend ran out of the room and she listened for the sound of the front door as it opened, and then finally when Anna heard the key locking the door she pulled herself out from under the bed.

She stood up and as she brushed the dust off her clothes, she let out a series of sneezes into the crook of her elbow. She waited a couple of minutes before she exited the apartment, ensuring Logan's girlfriend enough time to make it out of the building. She reached for the handle on the front door when the alert buzzed on her phone.

Someone was in her apartment.

CHAPTER 6-

By the time Anna returned home, the intruder, whoever they were, was long gone. She did a cursory sweep of the apartment and didn't notice anything missing or disturbed. That could only mean one thing. That something was left behind. She activated her music playlist on her stereo and turned up the volume while she checked the rest of the apartment.

Anna lifted the candlestick holder on the sideboard next to her table and extracted a long cylindrical-shaped object. She pressed the black button on one end of the unit and the opposite end came to life with a red blinking light.

Anna walked around the apartment, making her way from the back corner of her bedroom, ending her scan at the furthermost point in the kitchen. When she was finished, she had located two GSM listening devices.

They weren't elaborate spy devices, however, if they were placed in her apartment then whoever placed them there was on some sort of covert operation. She suspected there was probably one placed in her car as well.

Anna activated the monitoring devices in her apartment from her phone. All the units were still in place and were missed by whomever the intruder was.

She booted her computer to life and flipped over the mouse pad that had a scanning pad on the bottom. She placed the individual listening units on the pad one at a time and began to scan the units for prints. It wasn't likely that she was going to be able to pick up a print from the units, but it was worth the try. The scan was completed and although Anna couldn't lift any prints, she was able to retrieve a serial number. She made a note of the number and then turned off her computer.

She replaced the listening devices to the places where she found them and decided it would be best to leave the units undisturbed in her apartment. Someone was intent on watching her, and it was probably best to let them think they succeeded.

Anna tucked the scanning wand in her pocket and made her way to her car which was parked on the road. She always parked in an area with a great deal of foot traffic on the street, she figured it kept the chance of a car break-in to a minimum. Now she wished she had a more secluded spot to inspect the car.

As she approached the car, she intentionally dropped her keys on the road behind the car. As she bent to pick them up, she quickly dropped to the ground and got a quick glance at the undercarriage of the car. She didn't expect an explosive device, but she also didn't expect to have her apartment bugged either.

Once she was sure it was safe, she unlocked the car with her remote and slipped through the driver's door as the traffic buzzed by on the street.

A quick scan revealed that nothing seemed to be out of place in the interior of her car. She started the car and pulled out of the parking spot and made her way to the vacant lot near the river path that she often would jog along.

If she was being tracked, it was a common destination that she would make, and it would also give her the privacy to finish her scan of the car. She arrived at the lot and parked with the front of the car facing the entrance. She waited, pretending to read a book while a young couple piled their two dogs in the back of their SUV, and then watched as they made their way out of the lot and down the road.

When they were out of sight, Anna got to work and quickly scanned the car with the wand and after a few minutes found one listening device that was tucked under her steering wheel column. She reached into her bag and pulled out a piece of clear film that was affixed to a shiny whiteboard and slowly peeled it away.

She carefully lay in on the base of the steering column and hoped that the awkward and restrictive space in the car caused an errant fingerprint to be left.

Anna ran her gloved hand over the top of the film and pressed it into the plastic cover and then slowly peeled it away. She held it up to the light and smiled as the film revealed not one but two perfectly clear prints.

She reattached the film onto the glossy whiteboard and then returned it to her bag. She wondered who had placed the listening devices in her car and home. She knew it wasn't William and they weren't advanced enough for them to be from Alastair.

She stepped out of her car and placed a call to the private cell number William gave her during their last meeting.

William answered on the second ring.

"Anna, how did your trip go?" William asked.

"Good. Your intel on his routine was good and I was able to set up the bugging devices where I needed to." Anna said.

"So, I am assuming there were no problems," William said.

"Sort of. The girlfriend doubled back for her hospital pass, but I was able to get hidden quickly enough," Anna explained.

"That's why I brought you in. I needed your skillset, Anna," William gushed.

"Ha, nice William. No need to go there, I am already committed," Anna laughed.

"Have you got anything on the phone yet?" William asked.

"No, not yet, I just returned home, and I found something unexpected in my apartment," Anna said.

"What exactly?" William asked. Anna could hear the noise behind William fade followed by the sound of a door closing, leaving Anna to assume William found a more private location to speak.

"Three listening devices. Two in my apartment and one in my car," Anna explained to William. "Not very elaborate, but it still means someone's tracking me."

"Any idea of who it may be?" William asked.

"I was hoping you may have an idea. Who knows I'm helping you?" Anna asked.

"No one. Just like we agreed," William paused for five seconds. "Are you sure they were put there recently?"

Anna decided not to tell William about the scanning devices she placed inside her apartment before she left.

"I scanned the apartment before I left town and there was nothing there." Anna hating lying to William, but she didn't want him to think she pulled anyone else in. He managed to stay alive for the last couple of years, and she wasn't about to risk losing him again.

"Were you able to get any prints off of the devices?" William asked.

"No, they were too small to grab any, but I did notice they're older listening devices," Anna explained. "I think I got a couple of prints from my car though."

"Good, get those to me and I'll trace them and why don't you leave the listening devices in place, and maybe we can keep whoever is tracking you in a holding position," William suggested.

"That's what I was thinking, too." Anna was happy to be working with William again, and she didn't mind letting him take the lead. He always had great instincts and she trusted them.

"I'll send them to you once I am back home." Anna ended the call and returned to her car.

She started the car and began to drive back to her apartment. She took the same route back, making note of any cars or people she may have seen on the way out earlier. She made it back to her apartment and booted up her computer ensuring a secure connection as she uploaded the prints to the location William instructed. As she watched the progression of the transmission, she remembered the serial number on the devices and remembered she had failed to mention those to William.

She was about to send it along to William when she thought of Alastair. She trusted him with her life, and she knew that he had access to more equipment than William did with his limited resources now that he was undercover. She keyed up the secure connection app Alastair had installed on her computer and logged in.

After she typed a short explanation, she uploaded the prints and the serial number for the listening devices and hoped that Alastair would be able to get some useful information.

She reached into her back pocket and grabbed her phone and plugged it into the computer. She began to download the information she retrieved from Logan's exercise tracker as well as all the information from Logan's phone. Anna counted on Logan plugging his phone into the bugged outlet in his apartment when he returned home from work. She was satisfied to see that he had done just that. She loved it when people were predictable, it made her job so much easier. As she began to download the software, she noticed that he had quite a bit of information stored on his phone and all of it was being accessed by the remote software scanner she placed in the electrical receptacle in his home.

Anna left her computer and decided to unpack and take a shower. She let the hot water run over her head for a full ten minutes before she began to shampoo. The steam filled the room and she could feel the tension that built up in her shoulders ease under the stream of water.

When she felt relaxed enough, she turned off the water and reached for a towel hanging on the wall near the tub. She towel-dried her hair and dressed in her favorite pair of faded jeans and a white t-shirt. She pulled her head through the neck of her old grey sweatshirt from the academy and went to the kitchen to make herself a sandwich.

She walked over to the couch and plopped down with her sandwich and watched as the progress bar for the download was at 87%. By the time all of Logan's information had downloaded, Anna had finished her sandwich and was sitting at the computer ready to read the file.

At the same time, an alert buzzed on her computer screen from Alastair.

He typed, "Interesting update Anna. . . as always I am here to help. Glad you used my home connection since everything you are doing is under the radar there."

Anna answered, "Thanks, Alastair. I knew I could trust you and frankly, I didn't think anyone else would be able to handle this as quickly."

Alastair, "You know flattery will get you everywhere with me!"

Anna smiled and then typed, "What did you find?"

"Well, the listening device was easy. It is from the dark ages of spy technology. 1990 to be precise. I came across these a lot when we went in to help the Latvians after the border treaty was signed with Russia in 2007. They have been found in other countries, used by other agents as well, so not sure who is responsible for placing them on you."

"How about the serial number?"

"Government-issued, and as you can imagine the Russians have their own set of techie gurus protecting stuff on their end. I'll dig a little more on those."

"Anything on the prints?"

"They haven't been registered anywhere, but I'll keep trying."

"Thanks, I appreciate it."

"No problem, let me know if there is anything else and I will keep working on those prints."

"Will do. Oh, and thanks for your security bugs, they came in handy."

"Glad to help."

Anna closed the dialogue box with Alastair and began to read the files she downloaded from Logan's phone and exercise tracker.

She could tell by his tracker that he must jog the same route every evening, and judging by his chart he was fast. She also noticed he never wore it during the day at work, probably an agency policy. The CIA was well known for their paranoia, and as she sat at her computer reading Logan's devices, she knew they had a good reason to be.

The only time he seemed to wear it during the day was either on the weekends and the days he traveled for business. She began to scan the information from his phone and stopped when she noticed a travel itinerary that he recently downloaded. He had boarding passes for a flight he had booked that was leaving tomorrow.

She had the flight number along with the row and seat he was booked on. Anna stepped onto her balcony and closed the sliding door behind her. She picked up her phone and began to dial the number to a travel agent, who picked up on the first ring.

"Hello, Worldwide Travel Consultants, how can I help you?" The friendly perky voice answered.

"Hi, yes, I need a ticket leaving tomorrow for Latvia. I'd like to be on flight KLM 6760, please," Anna requested. "It's a family emergency."

"Oh, I'm so sorry to hear that," the agent said. "Let me see what I can find."

Anna patiently waited for the agent to come back on the line.

"Thanks for waiting, there are still some seats available on that flight, would you like to book one now?" the agent asked.

"Yes, please," Anna answered. "If you can, I'd prefer an aisle seat anywhere behind row 17." Anna wanted to make sure she could keep an eye on Logan all the way to Riga. After the agent confirmed her flight and seat reservation, she re-entered her apartment and went directly to her bedroom to pack.

CHAPTER 7–

It had been years since Anna was in the eastern region of Europe, and when she was, it was with Denis. They were completing a year-long operation following a human trafficking ring that stemmed from Turkey. They were able to track the flow of people into Europe through Bulgaria, but that did little to solve the problem higher up. They knew they were dealing with a highly organized group because no matter how many transports they intercepted or seized, they were unable to find the origin of the operation.

Their gut instincts told them government officials were involved and they knew they had to be smarter and faster if they were to make any difference in the lives of these people. A break in the case came when Denis was able to convince the mistress of Mr. Demir, a Turkish ministry official in charge of border security, to plant a bugging device on him. They were also able to enlist the help of her brother who was a member of a medical aid group working in the country. He was frustrated and concerned because so many people were dying or being killed while being transported out of the country.

Other governments had a feeling that the current administration was turning a blind eye to the illegal transportation of refugees out of Turkey since it would also solve their refugee problem. There were even rumors that government officials received payments to leave certain designated routes unsupervised.

Their chance came when they were sitting in a safehouse in Kapitan Andreevo, Bulgaria near the border crossing at Kapikule. They received word that a transport truck was expected to come across the border just after midnight and on it were documents stashed by insurgents proving the government's involvement in the human trafficking ring. The government official's mistress drugged him on an evening they were together, and she made copies of emails that provided a link to the government's involvement and she delivered them to her brother.

Anna and Denis were waiting at the border with officials from Bulgaria and when it was time, the guards at the border crossing were switched out with undercover agents, and the transport was captured just as it passed over the border. The documents were exactly where they were supposed to be, and they took great pleasure in handing them over to the UN to deal with the government officials involved. Within a week news came that the mistress and Mr. Demir were killed in a car accident and since the Turkey government claimed he was acting alone, the UN had no choice but to drop the case because they wouldn't be able to connect the evidence any further.

Bulgaria had since installed a border wall and the medical doctor that Denis was working with disappeared. Denis and Anna were told their mission was and they were instructed to return home.

Anna remembered that Denis was particularly upset, and on their last evening in Sofia, he found himself at the bottom of a large bottle of rakia. The Bulgarian brandy relaxed Denis's emotions and he volleyed between sadness and anger as he lamented their inability to help the innocent refugees, especially the children. Just before he passed out, she remembered him saying that no child should be left alone in a war-torn zone. It was the first glimpse that Anna had into the unhappy childhood that Denis may have experienced, but she never had a chance to ask him about it. A year later he was dead.

Now Anna was on a flight that was landing in Riga tracking an agent from her own government, and she didn't even really know why. The flight and connection through Frankfurt were uneventful, which was a good thing in her line of work. She broke the monotony of the flight by studying the town map of Riga and learning some key phrases in Latvian assuming the knowledge would be useful.

She learned over the years to pack light, and as she pulled her small bag from the overhead compartment, she was grateful. While Logan waited for his luggage to be unloaded from the plane, Anna went to the front of the airport where her rental car was waiting by the curb, just as she had arranged. The excruciatingly slow process the airline took in unloading the passenger's bags from their flight offered her the time to sync up her phone to Logan's exercise tracker while she waited.

She watched in her rear-view mirror as Logan walked out of the airport and into the first cab waiting in the cue at the side of the curb and followed behind them at a safe distance. She followed the red cab along the *Lielirbes iela* route straight into the central district of Riga. Anna had hoped Logan would not choose an uber since she was counting on the same route all cab drivers took to the town center.

Logan had booked himself into the Grand Hotel Kempinski, the most expensive accommodations in Riga. Anna preferred a more low-key accommodation when she was on assignment, however, most government agents like Logan took advantage of the travel budget and usually tried to live above their means while on business. Anna booked an Airbnb directly across the street from Logan's hotel which offered a direct sightline to his room and the front exit of the hotel. Anna monitored Logan's tracker from her phone and was reviewing the city map when she was alerted of his movement. She quickly made her way to the street level just as he exited his hotel.

This time Logan decided to walk and Anna pulled her cap down shielding her forehead as she followed behind at a safe distance. He wove his way through the streets of Riga revealing a tourist's knowledge of the city that would only come with frequent trips. He stopped at a street vendor that was selling flowers and began speaking to the old woman who was perched on a stool behind her mountain of assorted bouquets. Anna held back pretending to look in a shop window as Logan completed his purchase. The old woman handed him a bouquet of purple and white flowers as Logan folded several bills and pressed them into her hand. She grabbed his hand with both of hers and was thanking him profusely as he smiled and thanked her for the flowers.

Logan continued walking along Brīvības bulvāris until he reached the rotunda where the Freedom Monument stood. A few people were gathering around the monument, some took pictures, some reading pamphlets, some crying, and others placing flowers, as Logan was doing now.

Anna knew the significance of the Freedom Monument in Riga and what it represented to the people of the country, but as she glanced up at the 138-foot monument and squinted at the sun's reflection off of the three gold stars at the uppermost part of the statue, she was confused why Logan was placing flowers at its base.

He stayed only a moment before he continued through town walking in the direction of the Daugava River. He reached the Riga Cathedral fifteen minutes later and maneuvered his way through the crowd in the plaza and walked up the front steps. The red brick building cast a shadow on the plaza and Anna wove her way through the crowd of tourists as she followed Logan into the cathedral.

Anna extracted some bills from her pocket and slipped them in the slot at the entrance and took the pamphlet handed to her by the ticket agent. Logan slipped into a pew on the far side of the church and she positioned herself behind a pillar as she observed his movements.

He was against a stone wall and pulled out the visitor pamphlet and distracted himself with it until a few moments later a man about the same height as Logan sat next to him. The man's features were obscured and Anna moved to the other side of the pillar to get a better view. When she reached the other side of the pillar, she held her phone camera up and pretended to be focusing on the stonework above where Logan and the mystery man were sitting on the bench. As Anna watched through her lens, she snapped pictures of the man handing Logan an envelope but was still unable to catch a clear view of his face.

Logan stood to leave and the man exited the bench in the opposite direction. The man he was meeting with was gone, but Anna needed to stay on Logan's trail and she followed him out the front of the church.

This time Logan walked only a few blocks until he arrived at a small local restaurant. Anna watched from across the street as Logan entered and greeted the man at the door with a hug. They closed the old wooden door behind them, and Anna could see through the wavy glass window the movement of their bodies toward the back of the building.

Anna ran across the street and moved along the side of the stone building in a low crouch until she reached the back door. She squatted behind a bush just as the back door opened and a middle-aged woman emerged and headed toward a line of parked cars behind the building. While the woman was preoccupied with trying to locate her keys at the bottom of her oversized bag, Anna shoved her hand between the door and the frame and caught it when it was inches from closing. She pushed it open just far enough to slip through and then let it close behind her.

The inside of the building was dark, but what struck Anna was the damp, moist odor of the old stone building mixed with the aroma of cooking that emanating from the kitchen in the back. The sweet, pungent smell filled the hall and struck up a reminder in Anna's stomach that she hadn't eaten since the plane landed.

Anna moved along the old tile floor with her back pressed against the wall. There was a mirror in the hall next to her, and she could see the Logan in the reflection.

"Here's the documentation we agreed upon," Logan said as he slid an envelope on the table to the man sitting across from him.

"And the wire transfer? Has that been done?" the man sitting across from Logan asked.

"When the job is completed, Dr. Petrov, just as we agreed," Logan explained.

"I told you not to use my name!" the man snapped as he leaned in close to Logan.

Logan put his hands up in defense, nodded, and yelled, "Prosti."

Russian! Anna didn't remember anything in Logan's file about him speaking Russian.

Logan then asked, "And the formula?"

The doctor then reached into his pocket and extracted a small vial filled with an amber liquid and he then handed it to Logan. Just then a clattering of pots reverberated from the kitchen along with a scream from the lone staff member that remained in the room.

Still watching from the reflection in the mirror, Anna saw a man vaulting over the bar counter and landing a few feet from where Logan was sitting with Dr. Petrov.

As the man landed, he held a gun pointed at the table area and directly at the two men. Anna slipped her gun from her holster and pressed her back against the wall as she moved closer to the open room, all the while keeping an eye on the gunman.

"Kur ir flakons? Where is the vial?" the gunman shouted at Logan and Dr. Petrov.

"I don't know what you are talking about?" Dr. Petrov said. Anna could see him reach for the gun he had on his lap under the table.

As the gunman turned to face Logan, Dr. Petrov flung his left arm from under the table and pulled the trigger three times. The second and third shots hit the right side of the gunman's body knocking him off balance, but only for a moment. He quickly aimed his gun at Dr. Petrov and with one fatal shot sent Dr. Petrov's body backward and he hit the floor with a thud. The gun fell from his left-hand tumbling under the table and landing near Logan's feet.

Anna jumped from behind the wall and fired a series of shots at the gunman just before she dove behind a post. The gunman's bullet blasted the mirror behind her sending shards of glass flying at her head, and a few more shots ricocheted off the edge of the post and then one shattered the front window drawing the attention and screams of people on the street. She fired another shot at the gunman's leg, and he shrieked as he fell to the floor.

Logan dove for Dr. Petrov's gun that had landed near his feet and after a momentary glance at Anna he reached into Dr. Petrov's pocket and retrieved the envelope he had given him only a short while earlier and raced out the door.

"Damn it!" Anna couldn't lose him. She stepped out from behind the post just as the gunman aimed his weapon in Logan's direction and she raised her arm pulled the trigger. The gunman fell backward with the force and landed in a crumpled heap on the floor.

Anna took off after Logan and burst out of the front door and chased off after him down the street. She pushed through the screaming crowd that started to build in front of the restaurant. She could see Logan as turned right at the end of the cobbled street and Anna took off after him.

Logan reached the plaza next to the Cathedral and pushed through the crowd of people as he ran. Anna chased after him and ducked around an old woman and jumped over a bench as she began to close in on him.

"Pietura! Policija!" Anna heard yells calling from behind and to the side of where she was running. She stopped at the police officer's command and watched as Logan disappeared around the corner.

Anna turned to see a policeman approaching her with his gun raised in his shaking arm. She lifted her hands and turned slowly to face the officers. She counted three, each with their guns pointed directly at her.

She moved cautiously and lowered her gun to the ground and turned slowly as the policemen moved in. A crowd of people began to run from the commotion that was building around Anna not wanting to catch a stray bullet.

She moved her feet slowly as she turned in a small circle, watching each step the officers made remembering a similar drill from training.

As the officer behind her grabbed her right shoulder she swung her left hand over his, pulling his arm forward and twisting it above her head, turning her body as she pulled him toward the ground.

She sent a right roundhouse kick into the second officer's chest sending him tumbling backward landing on the cobblestone plaza, and while still gripping his arm, she jumped over his body and flipped him on his face, and twisted until she heard a pop, stopping just before the breaking point.

He lay writhing in pain as the third officer jumped toward Anna. As he lunged at her she twisted her right shoulder into his arm, blocking his swing and she simultaneously landed a punch in his gut. He swung with his right arm toward her head and she threw up her left arm blocking his swing and wrapped her hands around the back of his neck and jammed her knee into his head, rebounding him backward.

With the three officers subdued, Anna stooped down to pick up her gun and took off after Logan in the direction she saw him leave. She cursed herself for losing him and drawing the attention of the police and hoped she hadn't lost too much time in the plaza. She pulled out her phone and pressed the app that brought the location of Logan's exercise tracker online. She followed the curved line to where it reached a point near the river.

She saw the Vansu bridge ahead to her left and knew that Logan was running across it. From reviewing Logan's running stats on his exercise tracker, Anna knew that he often took walking breaks every half mile. She counted on Logan losing steam and at the same time, she began to run as fast as she could to catch him.

She could feel the burn in her thighs as she pounded along the pavement and reached the bridge. The gun began to slip in her waistband, but she couldn't take another chance at grabbing it and drawing any attention running down the street while holding a gun.

Logan turned right as he reached the end of the bridge and he headed directly toward a green field and she could see he was heading into a cemetery. Anna took a quick left and headed to the fence surrounding the cemetery property and cleared it with one jump. She was able to make her way around the faded and broken gravestones to come out from behind a clump of crooked trees right in front of Logan.

Logan stopped in mid-stride almost falling sideways.

He was panting heavily, and Anna could see the color rising in his cheeks as he stood to face her. She imagined his exercise tracker was binging like crazy right now.

"Stop Logan! I'm not going to hurt you, I just need to talk to you," Anna held both of her hands up to show him she didn't have a gun in them. "See, I just want to talk." Anna took a step closer to Logan.

"Stay there! Don't move!" Logan screamed.

"Okay, Logan. You're going to be alright," Anna took another step and stopped.

"Who are you? How do you know my name?" Logan asked through gasps of air.

"I'm an agent in the U.S. government, we are on the same side. At least I hope we are," Anna said. "Who is Dr. Petrov and why were you meeting him?"

"How do you know about Dr. Petrov?" Logan took a step backward on the path, moving away from Anna.

"I heard you in the restaurant. I need to know what you were meeting about and what's in that vial," Anna asked.

"It's not what you think," Logan said.

"What do I think Logan?" Anna asked.

"I'm on the good side. You have to believe me," Logan begged.

Anna took another step closer to Logan and suddenly a gunshot fired from behind her head and hit Logan square in the chest and at the same time, a kick landed in the middle of her back and it sent her falling to the ground.

She landed on the pavement and turned over on her back to face her attacker. From the build, she could tell it was a man, but other than that his features were obscured by the balaclava he was wearing. She kicked her legs up surprising her attacker, grabbing the center of his legs and twisted them with full force sending him crashing to the ground.

He flipped his body releasing his legs from her grip and brought his right leg down on her ribs, feeling them crack under his boot. She screamed as the pain shot up her side.

She tried to reach for her gun, but he was able to slip his hand behind her back and pull the gun out of her waistband and held it pointed at her as he stood.

Without a word, he walked back toward where Logan was laying on the edge of the path. He had managed to crawl only a few feet before the attacker reached him. Logan moaned in pain and Anna could see the trail of blood from where he crawled. The attacker knelt and with one hand holding the gun on Anna, he slipped the other inside Logan's coat and took out the envelope, and then rooted around a little longer until he also found the vial.

Anna held her breath and contracting her muscles she burst up from the ground lunging at their attacker.

She grabbed the gun just as he squeezed the trigger sending the bullet over her head. She pulled his arm toward her as her left knee landed on his face and she could feel the sound of his nose breaking under the cover of the balaclava.

He grabbed her leg and pulled it up and threw Anna to the ground knocking the wind out of her lungs and sending fresh shots of pain through her ribs.

She kicked her right leg on the outside of his body sending him to the ground with a thud. She climbed on top of him jamming her knee into his chest and she reached into his pocket to retrieve the envelope and vial. He grabbed her hand and twisted it from his pocket just as she was about to touch the envelope and twisted it around. She grabbed his arm with her right hand and peeled his thumb back until it cracked, scratching at his arm as she loosened the top of his glove.

The hit came to the side of her head and her vision began to fade. She fell to the ground just as Logan yelled out and she caught a glimpse of the familiar tattoo and then it all went black.

CHAPTER 8-

Anna awoke to a throbbing ache on the side of her head and along the edge of her rib cage. She looked directly into the face of an older woman who was standing above her, brushing her hair away from her face and asking her if she was okay.

An elderly couple had stumbled upon Logan and Anna sprawled on the ground and was trying to find out what happened. They were nervously asking her if she was hurt and were pointing at Logan's lifeless body as it lay crumpled next to a headstone.

Anna pretended not to speak Latvian and grabbed her cap as she stumbled to her feet and pushed by the gentle couple and toward where Logan lay. She checked his pulse even though she was sure he was dead and then slipped her hand into his inside jacket pockets until she located his hotel room card. She continued to look for his wallet and removed it as well, figuring it would buy her some time if the authorities couldn't identify the body immediately.

The couple was clamoring around her, trying to get her to speak to them. Instead, she put her cap on her head and then made her way to the cemetery gates, leaving the confused couple behind.

Anna pulled her cap down low on her head to shield her eyes and with her chin tilted down, made her way back to the hotel and left the poor couple to deal with Logan's lifeless body.

She knew they would be calling the police, and after her recent altercation in the plaza, she knew that she wouldn't be given the benefit of the doubt.

She managed to make it across the bridge just as the police and ambulance screeched toward the cemetery. Searing pain shot up from her broken rib and each step sent a new wave of pain up her back. Her labored breathing was beginning to make her lightheaded and she focused hard on the road in front of her.

She made it the remainder of the distance to the Airbnb without drawing any attention to her injuries and was thankful for not having to pass too many people on the way.

Walking up the steps to the apartment was more painful than she had expected. It had been a while since she had a broken rib and had forgotten how painful it could be. She made sure to open and close the door with her left hand only, preserving the skin under her nails the best she could. She kicked the door closed behind her and went to the kitchen and pulled open three drawers until she found one containing sandwich bags and pulled one out of the box and brought it into the bathroom.

Anna dropped it on the counter and with one hand managed to pull out a bag and open the zip lock closure and stood it up behind the taps. She then opened her toiletry bag and removed her tweezers.

She carefully unscrewed the rubbing alcohol she found in the medicine cabinet and poured it over the tweezers and shook them dry. She then scraped the skin under her nails from where she dug at her attackers' arm. She dropped the skin samples in the bag and zipped it closed and hoped they were big enough to run a DNA test.

Once she placed the bag in the next room, she removed her shirt and stepped in front of the mirror. Anna turned her body to examine her ribcage and noticed the bruising beginning to rise to a deep purple on the surface of her skin. She turned the cold water tap on full and let it run while she held a cloth under the stream.

She pushed the cold wet cloth against her side and cringed at the sharp pain. She then turned her head sideways and saw a trickle of blood rundown behind her ear. She pulled back her hair and was faced with another bruise and a bump, but she was glad to see she didn't require any stitches.

She didn't have many options now. Logan was her only lead and it took William a full year to narrow his search down to him. Anna cursed herself for leaving herself vulnerable in the cemetery and allowing the attacker to get away with both the envelope and the vial.

She figured she had a bit of time before Logan's handlers found out he was dead. She walked over to the window and looked out at the hotel across the road and figured she had less than twenty minutes to get in and search his room.

Anna dug around in her toiletry bag and pulled out a bottle of painkillers. She unscrewed the cap and knocked three into the palm of her hand and then swallowed them down with a glass of water. She then put on a dark sweater and left the apartment.

Anna entered the hotel as she pulled out her cell phone pretending to be on a call as she made her way to the elevator bank, shielding her face from the hotel security camera.

She continued to speak into the phone with her head held down until the elevator doors closed. She pressed the button for Logan's floor with her knuckle and rode the rest of the way up taking short quick breaths suppressing the pain in her ribs.

The elevator buzzed when they reached the floor and Anna stepped out into the hall. She walked by the chambermaids with her head tilted down and scanned Logan's card at his room. As she pushed open the door Anna placed the 'do not disturb' card on the outside handle of the door and locked the door as it pressed close. Logan hadn't been in his room long and his suitcase still lay closed on the end of the bed, next to the laptop case he carried on the plane. Anna unzipped the bag and removed the computer. Once she pressed the power button, the computer blinked to life and Logan's secure password screen appeared.

Anna inserted the specially designed USB stick into the side of the laptop and pressed the circular button on the outside of the stick. The red light on the end of the stick blinked three times and then the sequence was initiated to read and download the entire laptop hard drive without the need to access Logan's security code.

The download was completed within seconds and when the light on the USB stick shone green, Anna pulled the USB stick out of the laptop and she shut the computer and returned it to Logan's bag. Just before she closed the bag and zipped it closed, she spotted a photograph that Logan had tucked into the mesh pouch inside the case. It was a picture of him and his girlfriend, taken somewhere on a beach, obviously while on vacation.

She felt a moment of sadness, knowing the grief that his girlfriend was going to feel once she was told that Logan was gone. Anna returned the bag to where she found it and slipped the USB stick into her pocket. She checked the drawers and Logan's toiletry case, but there was nothing to indicate what his business dealings were in Riga or what 'Seaforth' referred to. It was the word he yelled before he died, and she didn't know what it meant.

The hotel telephone rang as she was about to open the door. The red light flashed with each ring and Anna lay her hand on the receiver. Anna could tell by the prefix of the number on the screen, that the call was coming from inside the hotel. On the third ring, she lifted the receiver and held it to her ear, and listened.

"Logan! You're back!" a man exclaimed. The voice was deep and American.

Anna grunted, hoping it was convincing enough to sound like Logan.

"Good, meet me in the lobby and bring the package." The man disconnected the call and Anna replaced the receiver to the base.

Anna realized she got as much as she could from the room and knew it was time to leave. She looked out of the fisheye peephole on the door and when she was certain the hall was empty, she made her way to the elevator. She was able to keep her face shielded from the security cameras in the hotel and when she entered the lobby, she quickly scanned the room to see if she could figure out who had called Logan's room. At a quick count, Anna figured there were just under twenty people in the lobby and just over half of them were paired off as couples. She turned around and pressed against the door with her back, taking a glance around the room to see if there was any sign of the caller. She could tell by his voice that he was American, and by his inflection that he was from the mid-west.

Anna didn't recognize anyone waiting in the lobby but noticed one man sitting in a lobby chair, watching the bank of elevators as he tapped his foot. Judging by his stature he was five-ten and about one hundred and ninety pounds. She committed his light brown hair and eyes to memory along with the mole on his right cheek.

She decided it was best to return to the apartment and make it to her safehouse so she could contact Alastair. It was close to midnight and she found moving at night beneficial in this region. She was across the street when she felt her phone vibrate in her pocket.

She pulled it out of her pocket and on the screen the tracking device she installed to follow Logan's phone flashed to indicate it was moving. And it was heading toward the hotel.

CHAPTER 9-

It took ten minutes for Anna to grab her bag and be in the car heading toward the safehouse. It was located south-east of Latvia in the small town of Skaune, situated near the border of Belarus and Russia. It was a great location for her to have access to when on a covert operation for a couple of reasons. It was strategically located near areas she often worked undercover and close to the national park that bordered Russia and Belarus making her entrance into Russia almost undetectable. As well, the people from the region still remembered the suffering they endured at the hands of the Russians and often would turn a blind eye to any non-Russian in the region.

Anna waited until she was outside of the city limits before she pulled her phone out of her pocket and dialed William's number. She knew that the late hour was irrelevant and William picking up on the second ring confirmed that.

"Hello," William never answered the phone revealing who he was. And no matter what the incoming number was, he never assumed to know who was on the other end.

"It's me, William," Anna didn't know how to sum up the events of the day to William. He had worked so hard over the last two years. He took his life underground and ran a covert operation to uncover those involved with the explosion and the larger conspiracy.

"Anna, I didn't expect to hear from you so soon," William answered. "Is this good or bad?"

"Logan's dead William. I was able to follow him to a small restaurant where he had a meeting with a man that he called Dr. Petrov. He exchanged an envelope for a small vial that was filled with some amber-colored liquid. He also mentioned something about a wire transfer."

"What happened?" William asked.

"Well, it all happened so quickly. A gunman appeared from the back of the building. He was speaking Latvian, and he seemed to know what Logan and this doctor were meeting about and he was there for the vial. To make a long story short, shots were fired, and Logan grabbed the envelope and the vial and made a run for it."

"Then what did you do?" William asked.

"I, unfortunately, had to take out the Latvian, he had his gun aimed at Logan as was going to kill him," Anna explained. "I was trying to keep Logan alive William."

"I know. What happened then?" William huffed.

"I followed him to a cemetery and had cornered him. I almost had him. The vial and envelope were just in his pocket," Anna said remembering the moments before the attack.

"Then," William prompted Anna to continue.

"We were surprised by an attacker. I fought him off, but he ended up shooting Logan and getting the envelope and vial just before knocking me out," Anna explained.

"That doesn't sound like you, Anna. You could take a team of five guys," William said. "I've seen it."

Anna knew William was right and thought back to when the Latvian police tried to stop her in the plaza.

"That's the thing, William. This was no ordinary guy. Whoever he was, he had definite combat training and he knew what he was looking for," Anna said.

"Are you sure?" William asked.

"Yes, damn it! I'm positive," Anna yelled. "Whoever he was, he was a professional."

"Any idea where he was from? Did he speak? Did he have an accent?" William peppered questions at Anna through the phone.

"No, he didn't say a word," Anna answered, she decided not to mention the tattoo until she had a chance to run the skin sample. "Was there anyone else in the area from your group?"

William was silent for a couple of seconds. Not long, but long enough to make Anna realize he was thinking of what to say.

"No Anna. You are the only one I sent after Logan," William said.

"But before, did you ask anyone else?" Anna asked.

"No, I swear. I am just as confused as you are," William said.

"Do you trust everyone you brought in on this mission?" Anna asked.

"With my life," this time William didn't hesitate to answer.

"I may have been able to pull something from his computer, but I won't be sure until I can check it out. I pulled it on an encrypted stick, and I need to get my equipment at the safehouse to pull it off," Anna said.

"Are you going there now?" William asked.

"Yeah, I will be there in about four hours or so. I'll let you know if I can pull anything from it once I have had a chance to review it," Anna explained.

"Okay. I'll see if my contacts in Riga can find out who the two men in the restaurant were. I am sure the police were called to the restaurant if there were shots fired. I'll let you know what I find out. Be safe," William said before he disconnected the call.

Anna was sure there was something she was missing. She decided to focus on figuring out what she had missed as a way to keep awake during the long drive. Her head and side were beginning to ache and with her free hand, she dug the pill bottle out of her bag and twisted the cap, and tipped the bottle to her mouth until a couple of pills dropped onto her tongue. She swallowed them down with some water and took a deep breath as she prepared for the long drive ahead.

It took Anna close to four hours and as she was nearing her destination the sun was almost up. Anna figured Alastair should be waking up soon and dialed his personal number from her cell phone, so she could catch him at home.

"Hello," Alastair answered with the quick cheery iambic tone of his British accent.

"Alastair, it's Anna," it occurred to Anna she hadn't spoken with Alastair in close to a year. Any communications they had were done electronically.

"Well, Anna darling, how are you?" Alastair exclaimed.

"I've been better Alastair," Anna answered, still feeling the pain in her ribs. "Listen, I used that reverse download stick you gave me a few years back on a laptop last night. If I connect to your private server can you download it for me?"

"Sure, what are you looking for?" Alastair asked.

"Not sure actually. Maybe some chemistry files, or anything that is written in Latvian or Russian," Anna said. "Basically, anything other than cat pictures and family emails. The needle in the haystack search."

Anna thought back to the photo of Logan and his girlfriend tucked in the mesh pocket of his laptop case and wondered if she knew he was dead yet.

"Well, I have some good news for you then," Alastair said.

"Good, I could use that," Anna said.

"No news on the prints, but I did trace the bug in your apartment," Alastair said.

Anna had almost forgotten about her apartment being bugged.

"The serial numbers didn't come up that easily because they were contents of a box that was recorded as damaged," Alastair explained.

"Damaged? Damaged how?" Anna asked.

"They were confiscated from a Russian passage ship trolling Swedish waters about fifteen years back and the boat that was transporting them to international authorities at the UN had sunk on the way," Alastair explained.

"Who was transporting them back?" Anna asked.

"It was a U.S. boat," Alastair said. "But that is not the strange part."

"Really? What's the strange part?" Anna asked.

"I searched the boat's manifest and got the name of the crew members," Alastair said.

"Was there anyone you recognized on the ship?" Anna asked.

"Remember Anna, these are deeply classified files and I'm not even sure what they were doing on the boat in those waters in the first place," Alastair said.

"Who was on the list Alastair?" Anna gripped the steering wheel as another sharp pain jabbed her side.

"William's name was on the list," Alastair answered.

"There must be some mistake, Alastair," Anna said.

"I am sorry, I double-checked the file myself, and, well," Alastair hesitated before he continued.

"What Alastair?" Anna said.

"There was another person on that ship that you know," Alastair said.

"Just tell me, Alastair," Anna said.

"It was Juris Ledin, Anna. He was on the ship along with William," Alastair said.

The last name Anna would have expected to hear was her father's name. She pulled the car over to the side of the road and stared out the window.

"Are you certain Alastair?" Anna asked.

"Very," Alastair said. "Remember Anna, they participated in several covert operations. You don't know exactly what they were doing'."

"I know that Alastair. But how do you explain one of those devices ending up in my apartment?"

"I can't," Alastair said.

"And nothing on the prints?" Anna asked. She needed to make sense of what was happening.

"Not yet, but I'm working every contact I have to find out who they belong to," Alastair said. "I'll call you as soon as I know more."

"Okay. But I'm not home anymore," Anna said. "Just use this cell number okay."

"Okay. Where are you?" Alastair asked.

"Latvia."

"What are you doing in Latvia?" Alastair asked.

"Following a lead that William had," Anna explained.

"And how did that pan out? Any new intel?" she could hear Alastair filling his kettle with water in the background.

"Yes, and no," Anna said. "I am pretty sure this guy was up to something illegal, but I'm still not sure what exactly. He was killed last night."

"What? How did that happen? Was it you?" Alastair was always keenly interested in the details from the field, living vicariously through agent's missions since MI6 was never going to let him out of the office. He was too valuable there.

"No, it wasn't me. I was attacked by the guy who killed him," Anna said.

"Is your operation already over?" Alastair said

"I hope not. But listen, I need something else, too," Anna said thinking about the skin samples she had in her bag.

"Sure, what is it?" Alastair asked.

"I got some of the attacker's skin under my nails when I was fighting him. I want to have them processed," Anna explained.

"Well, I have someone close to where you are now that you can trust to run a trace," Alastair explained. "By the time you get them to me, he could have the trace processed."

"I don't know Alastair, I'm not sure I want to pull anyone else in. Especially, someone, I don't know," Anna was apprehensive.

"But I know him, Anna. And I trust him with my life, for so many reasons, and I should hope that would be enough," Alastair tried to reassure Anna.

Anna thought about it and then said, "Okay, who's your guy and where do I find him," Anna acquiesced. She knew she had to trust someone.

"His name is Sergey Pashkevich. I will send his contact information to your cell number," Alastair explained. "I will ring him and tell him to expect you."

"Okay, thanks Alastair," Anna said.

"No problem. Be safe," Alastair said.

Anna was about to disconnect the line when she thought of one more question.

"Oh, Alastair, what was the name of the ship that William and my father were on?" Anna asked.

"The Seaforth," Alastair said. "But it doesn't look like it's in service any longer.

Anna's jaw dropped as she ended the call with Alastair.

She pulled the car out onto the road and made her way the last five miles to the safehouse, determined even more than when she started.

CHAPTER 10-

The rim of twenty-foot tall pine trees that surrounded the safehouse was about a quarter of a mile deep and was the perfect cover for any vehicle you want to keep hidden from the sky or the ground.

Anna made the remainder of the way to the safehouse on foot. She wanted to make sure she wasn't followed and then she could be sure there would be no indication of her presence at the safehouse once she arrived.

The gentle buzz of her phone through the thick jean material of her coat came as Alastair sent the directions to Sergey's home along with his phone number. As Anna looked down at the phone, she saw the tip of her tattoo inching past the edge of her shirt sleeve. She pulled down her sleeve and put the phone back in her pocket.

She couldn't help but draw her mind back to when she was attacked in the cemetery and when Logan was killed. She remembered the tattoo, that she was sure of. But no matter how hard she tried to remember she couldn't think of any other features of the attacker to set him apart from the other people she was thinking about.

She tried to remember the group at the academy on the night they decided to get the tattoos. They had just finished their wilderness survival training and they were one step away from graduating. They had all made it through the toughest part of the training and with only two weeks left, they wanted to make the most of their time together.

It's true what you imagine about soldiers and agents that go through special training together. They bond closer than family. They become the people you must count on not only to work with but to put your life in their hands. It was Denis's idea that they get matching tattoos, he had always talked about the other agents as being his family.

Whenever Anna or the other agents would talk about their families, Denis was always silent about his past. One night after a few too many beers, Anna had asked Denis why he was so private about his past and he had just said he was forced to grow up tough and that he was left alone at a young age. He had also mentioned that everything depended upon him getting through his training.

Anna never questioned him again because it just seemed too painful for him and she wasn't sure if it was just the beer talking. She always thought they'd have more time together, but she was wrong. Now she was thinking of the others from the group who also got the same tattoos that night and tried to figure out which one could've been responsible for attacking her and killing Logan. There were five of them in total, and when they were in the academy, they were a tight-knit group. She knew she could rule out she and Denis, so that left three possible options.

Anna hadn't stayed in touch with any of the others after Denis's death. Her means of survival was to shut everything out and try and move on. That left Simon, Greg, and Peter. Of the three, Simon was the one that Anna pegged as the most likely suspect.

After graduation Simon got the most elite posting working directly with the top brass and answered to only one person – the President. Simon had a knack for making himself useful to anyone in power. Unfortunately, he also let the taste of his influence guide him into less than legal dealings with foreign governments.

Five years earlier, Anna and Denis were on an operation in the Baltic Sea when they found themselves under attack as they were closing in on their target. Anna and Denis had worked for eighteen months and had been days away from closing in on a huge drug and money laundering scheme lead by a coalition of Russian and Syrian mobs. Not only would have meant huge promotions for them, but they would also have been able to crack a ring that was infiltrating North America at an alarming rate.

It was too late when they realized Simon had used his influence and was working both sides and that he was the leak into North America. There was no one that Anna hated more than Simon. His cockiness and arrogance became clear after graduation, and he often risked other agent's safety to gain glory for himself. But Anna's feelings ran deeper than that for Simon, it was more than her not liking him, she learned to never trust him.

If Anna had to lay a bet, she would choose Simon to have been the one who attacked her, but she wanted to be sure first and to do that she needed to have the skin tissue tested. She approached the edge of the tree line and spotted the safehouse ahead. It was situated about five hundred yards from the edge of the forest and backed onto a large hill. The safehouse looked more like a weekend cabin with a wooden log house exterior, but it was what was on the inside that distinguished it from any ordinary weekend house.

The high-tech interior was a team effort on behalf of both MI6 and the CIA. The safehouse was outfitted with satellite relay technology, individual passcodes, secure untraceable wireless technology, had a steel interior frame and bulletproof windows, enough food for six months and it comfortably slept twelve.

It was designed in the event agents needed to disappear for a long period but still needed to stay in touch with their unit. William had a special working relationship with the head of MI6, Rupert Davis. Both had risen to the top of their field despite the hurdles others threw in front of them. They both faced narrow-minded thinkers and discrimination from within their own government units. William because he was black and Rupert because he was openly gay.

The thing that made both men so admired by their subordinates was that they never let their struggles affect how they treated anyone they worked with. Their intelligence, drive, and empathy were what made them great leaders and what keep their agents loyal to them. They were also prescient thinkers and laid the groundwork to prepare for advancements in technology and changes in political powers when they designed their agencies. That included bringing 'criminals' like Alastair on board.

The front of the safehouse looked like an ordinary wooden cabin, except that it wasn't. The solid wooden door was fitted with a two-factor identification system. If either one didn't work, the building was locked out and both agencies informed. The security system was designed so agents could gain entry even if they didn't have any identification with them. The use of a security card was ruled out since agents usually arrived with nothing but the clothes on their backs.

The first scan was located behind a wooden panel to the right of the front door. Anna moved her hand to the fourth panel up from the door handle and pressed it down until a soft mechanical sound whirled behind the wall and pulled the panel inwards and then it slid behind the siding revealing a glass screen. Anna placed her chin on the edge of the siding activating the red scan that moved from her chin to her forehead. A few seconds after the scan was complete, Anna was prompted to place her open palm on the panel.

The scan of her palm not only confirmed her prints but read the microchip implanted at the base of her thumb. The system unlocked, and the panel returned from behind the siding to conceal the security pad once more.

Anna reached for the handle on the solid wooden door and twisted it clockwise and pushed the door open. Inside to the left of the front entrance was a room where agents kept individualized lockers. Anna went to her locker and after she punched in her six-digit passcode, the lock clicked open and she pulled the door toward her.

Inside Anna kept a couple of changes of clothes along with her personalized laptop and special devices designed specifically for her by Alastair. She pulled out the small black case that held her laptop and closed the door shut pressing the red button activating the locking sequence.

Denis's locker was next to hers and she ran her hand over the keypad. She wondered if anything was left inside and if there was anything she should keep as a personal memento of him. She made a mental note to have Alastair reset the code, so she could remove some of his things later.

Anna grabbed her bags and walked into the living room and tossed them on the couch. She then dropped onto the chair and leaned her head back on the seat. She had to figure out how everything was connected. She closed her eyes and thought she should rest a bit before she began to plan how to make her way to Sergey's.

Just as she was drifting off to sleep, she heard a sound come from the next room. She jolted from her reclined position and sprang to her feet and walked steadily toward the direction the muffled sound came from. She walked cautiously moving toward the kitchen.

She began to reach for her gun that was tucked in the back of her waistband when he exploded through the door. She lunged at him from behind, slamming her boot into the back of his knee when he came through the door.

Anna dropped down and wrapped her arm around his neck, cradling his chin in her elbow and she pressed her gun against the back of his head.

She engaged the trigger and yelled, "Don't move."

He slowly placed both hands palm side up, "I won't. Anna, Put the gun down."

Anna took a closer look at the man laying on the floor.

His hair had changed color, but she could tell by the distinctive scar on the side of his jaw it was Simon.

"How did you get in here?" Anna was sure that Simon's password and scan credentials had been revoked.

"Calm down will you, I didn't know it was you," Simon began to get to his feet making sure he didn't make any sudden movements while Anna had the gun on him.

Simon knew that Anna was still furious about what happened, and he knew she wouldn't hesitate to shoot if she thought he was going to attack her.

"What are you doing here? I thought you were removed from the system," Anna said, still holding the gun pointed at Simon's chest.

"I was. But things have changed," Simon was breathing heavily and with his hands held up he indicated to Anna he was moving to the chair. "Look, I'm going to sit down, and you should too. I'll explain everything."

Anna motioned with the gun for him to sit in the chair she was in earlier, "Over there, where I can keep an eye on you."

"You look like you're in pain. Why don't you sit down?" Simon said.

"Don't worry about me. I'm fine," Anna snapped.

"Okay, suit yourself. You were always stubborn," Simon.

"It beats being a traitor," Anna snapped. She had never had a chance to confront Simon after his betrayal and there was so much anger in her right now, she didn't even know where she would start.

"I guess I deserved that one. But there are things you don't know about Anna. Things have changed," Simon explained.

"Lift your sleeve," Anna instructed.

Simon looked perplexed but yanked the shirt sleeve on his right arm up and revealed his entire right forearm.

"Not that one," Anna motioned the nozzle of her gun to his left forearm where their matching tattoos were placed.

"Anna, what are you doing?" Simon asked.

"Now!" Anna yelled and she could feel the pain in her ribs rise again.

Simon looked at Anna and slowly began to lift the sleeve on his left arm revealing his forearm. The tattoo had faded with time but apart from the burn he received on his first assignment out of the academy, there were no other marks on his skin.

Anna quickly grabbed his wrist and twisted it around, so she could see both sides of his arm. She lowered her gun and dropped her shoulders, she released his arm and it fell back onto his lap. She was sure she would see scratch marks from when she was attacked in the cemetery.

She walked over to the couch across from where Simon sat and fell onto the cushions.

"Why are you here Simon?" Anna asked.

"It's a safehouse. I am staying safe," Simon answered with a chuckle.

"I don't have time or patience for your games, Simon. I want to know why you're here," Anna held her gun flat on her lap.

"I was sent," Simon answered.

"By whom?" Anna asked.

Simon smiled, "William."

CHAPTER 11-

"Please tell me he is lying," Anna screamed into the phone.

"Anna, a lot has gone on in the last couple of years. I know you don't like Simon, but he's a great operative, and he's smart," William was trying his best to explain Simon's presence.

"It's not that I don't like him, it's that I don't trust him, and neither should you. He is a traitor William! How can you believe anything he says?" Anna asked.

"Because things have changed. I know you don't want to hear this, but I believe that Simon has changed," William was trying his best to convince Anna, even though he knew it would be a hard sell.

"You're right, I don't want to hear it," Anna snapped. "Simon will take the highest bidder. How can you be sure we can trust him?"

"Several years ago, Simon was in a tight spot. Let's just say he trusted the wrong bad guy," William began to explain. "He got between a ruthless dictator and a rogue group of insurgents who both wanted him dead. I had a team extract him from the Azao mountain range in Algeria just as he was about to be beheaded. He offered up his services to me for life. I have no doubt I can trust him because he knows I can drop him back in Algeria at any moment."

Anna paused trying to take in what William was saying. If it was anyone else, she would have questioned the veracity of the story, but because it was coming directly from William, Anna had no reason but to trust it. "How long has Simon been working with you?" Anna asked.

"For a little over a year. He has been working in secret for me ever since I had a suspicion that there was a leak from the inside," William explained.

"Why Simon?" Anna asked.

"Because no one would have believed it," William answered.

"That I can believe," Anna said. "So where do we go from here? I'm still not comfortable working alongside Simon."

"Listen, I understand Anna, but we are dealing with remarkable circumstances. I'm going to need you to do your best," William pleaded.

"Okay, but at the first sign that he is going off script, I'm done with him. Understand?" Anna said.

"Understood," William said. "Now where do we stand with the USB stick?"

"I am going to work on that once I get off the phone with you. I'll let you know if I find anything of use," Anna said.

"Okay, I'll wait to hear from you," William said.

"Alright, good night William," Anna said.

"Good night," William responded. "And Anna – thanks."

Anna ended her call and walked into the kitchen where Simon was waiting while she called William. Anna pushed open the kitchen door and was struck with the aroma of the stew that Simon had cooking on the oven. Anna hadn't realized how hungry she was until the moment she walked into the kitchen.

"Hungry?" Simon asked.

Anna just nodded and walked over to the table and pulled a seat back and sat down. She made sure it was a chair where she had a full view of the room, her instincts were still to not trust Simon.

Simon scooped up a couple of bowls and slid one in front of where Anna was sitting and placed a basket of bread in the middle of the table.

Simon pulled out a chair opposite of Anna and sat down in front of his bowl of stew and grabbed a slice of bread out of the basket and tore it in half and dunked it into the broth. He popped the soaked piece of bread into his mouth and chewed it back and after he swallowed, he nodded at Anna.

"Go on, I didn't poison it," Simon smiled, but Anna wasn't sure if it was his attempt at being genuine or if he was smirking.

Anna sniffed the bowl and plunged her spoon into the bottom scooping up a large serving. She ate the spoonful and had to admit it was pretty good. They ate in silence for about ten minutes until Simon was the one to speak.

"I was sorry to hear about Denis," Simon said.

Anna glared at Simon, "Really?"

"Look, Anna, I know what went down the last time we were together was, well, pretty bad. But it wasn't personal against you and Denis, it was just business. And I really had a lot of respect for you and Denis and I was really upset when the explosion took out William's operation," Simon said.

"It may have been business for you, but it was a little more for us," Anna said.

"I know it was bad business, but I have changed. You don't have to like me, but we should agree to work together to figure out who was behind the explosion," Simon said. "You have to admit, you know I can help."

Anna didn't fully trust Simon, but she knew that Simon had just the skills she needed to help. After her attack in Latvia, she was sure a backup wasn't a bad idea. "Okay, but I am not taking my eyes off you. Any sign you are stepping out of line," Anna said before Simon interrupted her.

"Yeah, I know. I am done," Simon smiled as she shook his head and he returned to his stew. Anna did the same and they finished the rest of their meal in silence.

When they were done, Anna pushed back her seat and stared at Simon. "Look if we are going to work together effectively, we both need to be honest with each other," Simon nodded in agreement and he began by explaining how he found himself in a precarious situation in Algeria and how William rescued him. He told Anna all he knew about the explosion and who could have possibly been behind it. Which wasn't any more than she already knew. Anna found out that it was Simon who had tracked down Logan and recorded his movements so Anna could track him.

The last twenty-four hours were the most revealing and possibly held the key to who was involved in the explosion.

"We need to extract the information I downloaded onto the USB from Logan's computer," Anna said. "Alastair is expecting me to upload the information onto the server in the back room."

"Then let's not keep Alastair waiting," Simon said as he straightened himself, pushed his chair back, and began to walk into the room adjacent to the living room that contained all the equipment.

The room had been completely wired and secured to prevent any unauthorized access. The entrance to the room was concealed with a secret panel that was built to the left of the fireplace. Simon placed his hand on the underside of the mantle and the pad scanned his hand for verification and then once his print was authenticated, the bottom of the mantle dropped a couple of inches revealing a veiled ledge underneath. After Simon pushed the hidden button just under the rim of the fireplace mantle a muted click of the latch releasing from behind the wall was followed by a soft whir of the panel and the wall was pulled back to allow Simon and Anna to enter the room.

It was important for the agents to have room to be able to access computer technology while they were off the grid. It wasn't as easy to do that now with the ever-changing upgrades in mainstream electronics. Even the standard encrypted drive or phone can eventually be traced by an elite government office. The command room, as the agents called it, was designed with a blend of two government technologies that kept a great check and balance system in place for all the agents.

Anna powered up the terminal in the center of the desk as Simon began to unlock the communications locker. The agents made it a practice to wipe their phones and trackers every time they made it back to a safehouse like this one to ensure that they were completely off the grid when they left and were back out in the field.

The green blinking cursor in the center of the black screen flashed three times before the screen lit up and the password protect prompt appeared. Anna entered her code and placed her palm on the mousepad which doubled as a security scanner.

Once Anna was able to access the network, she plugged the portable memory stick into the side of the computer and entered the key sequence to begin the download of the information directly onto Alastair's drive. As the download began the video link popped up at the bottom of the screen indicating that Alastair was online.

Anna clicked the box and Alastair's image expanded to fill the center of the screen. Anna smiled at Alastair as he greeted her with a warm smile.

"Morning," Alastair chimed as he lowered his head toward the screen. "How was the rest of your drive?"

"Good. I arrived safely. I began to download the memory stick onto your drive just now," Anna said.

"I saw that. That's why I called," Alastair said.

"Do you think it will take very long to decrypt the info?" Anna asked.

"Probably not," Answered Alastair. "Not to bad mouth your agency boy, but often these guys think they have blocked everyone out with a simple password or encryption program when they forget the ones who write those programs are usually at the ready to break into them."

Alastair gave a little chuckle then looked past Anna's shoulder and saw Simon standing in the room behind her.

"Is that who I think it is?" Alastair asked, sounding a little alarmed and confused.

"Yes Alastair, that's Simon," Anna answered. "Our friendly neighborhood spy."

"I thought he was persona non-grata?" Alastair whispered.

"Hello, Alastair! How is my British buddy?" Simon leaned over Anna's shoulder and faced the computer camera and looked directly at Alastair.

"I am not your buddy, and how did you weasel your way back in?" Alastair's tone was revealing. And from his tone, it was clear that Simon was not someone he chose to trust. Anna let a smile widen across her face.

"William brought me in," Simon said. "Why don't we all try and get along? Anna and I have agreed to."

"Only because I have no choice," Anna interjected as she pushed Simon aside with her right arm. "I don't like it either Alastair, but I need to trust William, so I guess Simon is in. For now," Anna shot Simon a glare that reminded him that she wasn't going to fall into line easily.

"When are you planning to head to Sergey's?" Alastair asked.

"As soon as I get the information off the drive and pack up a few essentials. I'm not sure where I'm going to be next and I want to be prepared," Anna explained.

Alastair could see Simon standing to the side but still within the listening range of their conversation. Alastair would have to wait to let Anna know what he found out since their last call. No matter what Anna said about William bringing Simon in, Alastair was not ready to trust him again.

Just then the echo of Alastair's computer beeping rang through the video call. Alastair turned his head to one of the many monitors he had to the side of his computer.

"Okay, I'm in," Alastair said. "Looks like a lot of useless standard agency info. Reports and stuff."

Alastair's brow furrowed as he scanned the screen. The information was flashing quickly, and Anna could see the reflection of the light as it changed across Alastair's face with each upload.

"This may be interesting," Alastair said. "I am sending you a couple of files that stand out here."

Within a couple of seconds, a file flashed across Anna's screen and Alastair's image was reduced to the top right corner of the screen. Anna looked at the file labeled 'Seaforth'. She understood why it stood out when Alastair came across it.

Anna double-clicked the file open and found subfolders that she proceeded to open. Located inside were banking documents that dated back over fifty years to various banks in Latvia. The files listed bank names, account numbers, and amounts that were transferred through many old and untraceable accounts.

"Woah," Anna exclaimed as she saw some of the figures. "How could this have gone unnoticed for so long?"

"Latvia has gone through so many political changes and invasions that each government added another veil of secrecy," Simon added as he was standing over Anna's shoulder scanning the documents she pulled up.

There were also files on numerous government officials. Anna clicked on a few of them and quickly read them and saw that they were dossiers on people they could easily have used in blackmail plans. There was everything. Murder, extramarital affairs, and government blackmail. Anna reduced the files and downloaded the entire batch back onto the memory stick. She wanted to have them available for later.

"Okay Alastair, thanks a lot. I think I need to check into some of these banks in Riga after I get a chance to meet up with Sergey," Anna said.

"Alright. Let me know how everything goes will you?" Alastair said.

"I will," Anna said. "Oh, one more thing. Is there any way you can unlock Denis's locker? I thought maybe I should go through his things now that," Anna couldn't bring herself to finish the sentence with 'he's dead'.

Alastair nodded, "Sure, I'll reprogram his code so you can open his locker with your passcode info.

"Thanks," Anna signed off her call and completed the copy of the files onto the memory stick.

As the files transferred to the memory stick she wondered what the connection to Seaforth was. She pulled the memory stick out of the computer and plugged it into her phone. She began to back up the information and password protected both the memory stick and the files.

When Simon was finished assembling their bags, he and Anna left the concealed area leaving the impenetrable room sealed off until the next time it was needed.

Anna and Simon went to separate rooms and began to pack for their trip to see Sergey. They had to pack light because most of their travel was going to be on foot and they had to be prepared to move fast.

Simon was waiting for Anna on the couch just a few feet from where they fought earlier. Anna nodded to Simon as she entered the room and said, "Let's go."

"I am ready when you are," Simon stood and slipped his arms through the straps of his pack and secured it to his torso. "Don't forget your passports. We are going to need our alternate identification if we need to travel on any mainstream routes."

Anna remembered the phenomenal shape Simon was in during their training and was always impressed with the stamina he could draw on when they were on long assignments. She also remembered he had a penchant for hiding secrets, along with weapons, from the agents he worked with and planned to keep a close eye on every move he made.

"I will meet you out front. I have to get some things first," Anna waited until Simon stepped out the front door before making her way over to the locker bay.

She had planned on grabbing her various passports that were stored in her locker, she didn't need Simon to remind her. Once she had removed her travel identification from her locker, she closed the door and opened Denis's locker.

She peered in and there weren't many items inside the locker. Anna reached in and pulled out a small brass pin he received on their graduation day from basic training. It was a personal gift from William and not the agency, and Denis had said it meant more to him than the official papers from the government. The second thing Anna grabbed was Denis's watch. He said it was a gift when he enlisted. Anna could never remember him being without it and wondered why it was here in the safehouse and not on his wrist during the explosion.

Anna was just about to close the door to the locker when she spotted a photograph tucked in the back of the locker. It was pushed as far back as the locker stretched, and if it had not been for the bent corner revealing the white underside, Anna would have missed it completely.

She pulled out a faded black and white photo of a family standing in front of a short stone wall that surrounded a small park that stretched out toward a beach-lined lake. There were five people in the photo, and it was reminiscent of times Anna shared with her parents in the summer months they spent at her grandparent's cottage at Lake-of-the-Woods in Northwestern Ontario. There were three young kids, two boys, and a girl. The photo looked to be about thirty years old and wore the telltale signs of having been carried around as opposed to having been safely tucked in a family album. Anna flipped the photo over and saw there was an address written on the reverse side that time had begun to fade.

She tucked the items in the front of her pack, except for the watch, which she had strapped on her wrist before turning to leave. When she joined Simon out front, she turned to face the security panel and proceeded to lock the safehouse as per the agency's protocol.

Anna and Simon walked in silence as they made their way under the cover of the densely treed forest toward the border, unaware that twenty thousand kilometers above them a satellite had engaged a tracking device and began to record their movements as they traveled toward Sergey.

CHAPTER 12-

Simon and Anna traveled the forested terrain of eastern Latvia in silence, only communicating about the path they should take for their route across the Latvian border and into Belarus. Simon had attempted to strike up a conversation a few times, only to be rebutted by Anna's terse replies or her less than subtle attempt at ignoring him.

Because of Latvia's strict regulations on wood harvesting, over fifty percent of the country's terrain consisted of impenetrable forests. A fact that Anna found made the path easier to traverse as they made their way across the eastern part of the country and planned to cross into Belarus undercover.

It was important that they were not spotted crossing the border and that they remain as well hidden as they possibly could. As they approached a crossing, they could hear a truck idling near the edge of the road.

Another benefit to the Latvian forestry regulation was their healthy export of lumber into Russia and Belarus. A lumber truck was parked by the edge of the road while the driver escaped quickly to take a break to relieve himself by the edge of the bushes.

Anna and Simon took the opportunity of the driver's distraction and made their way to the back of the truck. Simon pulled back the tattered white tarp covering the back of the truck bed and hoisted himself on the bed of the truck. Anna watched as Simon moved with such ease and strength that she couldn't help but be impressed with. Anna hoisted herself onto the back of the truck bed, ignoring Simon's extended hand when he offered it to her. Anna reattached the corner of the tarp to the edge of the truck frame and pulled off her backpack. She pulled out a small can of pepper spray from the side pocket and sprayed a line along the edge of the truck bed and then slipped it back into her bag. Simon then scrambled over the wrapped bundles of lumber until he was nestled behind the cargo unable to be seen by either the driver or inspectors, and Anna followed suit.

They figured it was at least a two-hour drive to the outskirts of Minsk. Simon offered to keep watch since he had a full night's sleep the evening before and knew that Anna was running on less rest. She hated to admit it, but she decided it would be a good time to get a bit of a break. She kept her backpack affixed to her shoulders and leaned into the corner of the truck bed. She hadn't slept since the flight into Riga and she was suddenly feeling a wave of exhaustion and the pain in her ribs had started to pulse against the weight of the pack she carried through the forest. The sound of the engine muted the thoughts in her head, and she was able to drift off to sleep.

She awoke to Simon nudging her boot with his, and when she opened her eyes, he had a finger pursed across his lips and he pointed to the rear of the truck. Anna straightened her back and listened to the footsteps outside the back of the truck. Most of the people in the rural areas speak Belarusian over Russian and the low tone of the voices indicated that the driver and border guard were familiar with each other. Anna was familiar with the border crossings, having used them in the past, and knew there were always search dogs at each station.

She could hear the voices of the driver and the patrol guard as they made their way around the vehicle, and as their conversation became clearer, she knew they were nearing the back of the truck. The sound of the dog chain rattling against the guard's leash was followed by the sound of the dog's claws as it perched its forelegs on the back of the truck bed. The animal quickly jumped back when it encountered the scent of the pepper spray that Anna sprayed along the rim of the truck. The guard and driver were immersed in a conversation about the latest football game that they didn't notice that the dog avoided the back of the truck altogether. The guard followed the driver back to his cab and after he climbed behind the wheel, waved him through the gate.

The slowing speed and frequent turns alerted them that they were nearing the outskirts of Minsk. The two stowaways made their way to the edge of the truck bed and pulled back the corner of the tarp and waited until the truck came to a stop at a corner before they jumped out onto the road.

Anna jumped first and was glad for the fact that Simon was behind her and couldn't see her face wince under the bolt of pain that stabbed at her side when her feet hit the ground. Once Simon was out of the truck, they made their way to the edge of the road and watched as the truck turned left.

"I remember a little of the city. I was here a while ago on assignment," Simon explained as he pointed toward a field. "Let's head that way. There is a small farm where I stashed a car and a local that owes me a favor."

Anna quietly followed Simon as he climbed a fence and began to walk across the field.

"What did you do that this local feels he owes you? Or do I want to know?" Anna asked.

"It's a she, and I just took care of a little domestic issue she was having with a boyfriend that was involved in an underground movement. His excessive drinking was attracting a little too much attention to their group and I helped her remove him," Simon explained.

Anna shook her head and followed Simon the rest of the way in silence. She pulled out her phone from her coat pocket and sent Alastair a message that they were within a short distance of reaching Sergey. She wondered if Alastair had any further success tracing any information on the Seaforth yet as well.

Anna watched as the flashing bubble moved along her phone screen indicating that Alastair was typing a text. It took a while, but the text came through.

"Seaforth was owned by a private security company. It was contracted out by the U.S. government for use in some surveillance operations. It took some digging, but the ownership was traced back to a company called Quantum Security. About four levels of numbered companies, but the principal of the main company was Steve Ashbury. You know – the same Steve Ashbury who was a Senator before he became Secretary of Defense."

Anna thanked Alastair and replaced the phone in her pocket and continued following Simon.

They reached the farm and Anna watched as the front door to the farmhouse swung open and a young dark-haired woman stepped out onto the lawn. She recognized Simon immediately and ran to greet him. She threw her arms around Simon's neck and held a long kiss as Anna looked on, uncomfortably.

Simon stepped back from the woman and with his arm around her waist turned to introduce Anna.

"Anna this is Tanya Kozlova," Simon pulled Tanya a little closer and it was obvious that they were more than just friends.

Anna extended her hand, "Hello, Tanya. I didn't know Simon had any friends." Anna laughed as she watched Tanya's face for any trace of familiarity.

Tanya was a beautiful woman. She had dark thick flowing hair and striking green eyes. She was incredibly fit and looked as if she could hold her own in a variety of situations.

"Yes, it's hard when you are always fighting for a cause to hold people close," Tanya responded.

Anna wasn't sure what story Simon had told her, but she didn't want to bother herself with that now anyway. She wanted to get the car as soon as possible and start to make their way to Sergey's. She needed to have the skin sample tested, it was the only clue as to who could be following her. Simon quickly changed the topic and told Anna the car was in the garage to the left of the house and told her he would meet her there in a couple of minutes.

"I just have some business to discuss with Tanya," Simon explained.

Simon headed back to the house with Tanya as Anna made her way to the garage. The garage had an oversized wood barn-style door that hung by a track along the top of the opening. Anna planted her feet and pushed the door open and it slid along the track as it made a squeaking noise from the rust that had built up over the time it had been exposed to the elements.

There was only one car parked in the garage and it was covered with a dusty tattered cloth. Anna grabbed the corner of the tarp and dragged it over the hood of the car and then gave it a final yank as it hung on the back truck. She rolled it up and tossed it in the corner of the garage and laughed as she shook her head. It was just like Simon to have a car like this. Anna was looking at a bright red ZAZ that was built around 1958. She hoped it ran better than it looked because, by the look of it, she would be surprised if it started.

"What do you think?" Simon walked up behind Anna as she was assessing the car.

"Couldn't find anything smaller? Or brighter?" Anna asked.

"What's wrong with it?" Simon laughed as he walked over to the driver's door and yanked it open with a creak.

"It's a bit small. Do you think it'll run?" Anna asked as she slipped into the passenger seat.

"Of course, it will! It's a supermini," Simon laughed as he started the car and put it in gear. As he slipped out of the garage and wove his way around the potholes in the gravel driveway, he waved goodbye to Tanya as she stood on the front lawn. Anna nodded her head to Tanya and watched Simon as he returned her smile.

Anna punched Sergey's address that Alastair gave her into her phone's GPS and watched as the screen produced a map to follow from the farm to Sergey's location. Anna was still trying to figure out how to give the sample to Sergey without letting Simon know that she had it or what she was searching for. She hadn't told William about the skin sample she removed from under her nails either and she wanted to keep that information from Simon as well.

It took approximately twenty minutes to reach Sergey's apartment near the center of town. Sergey was located near Victory Square just steps from the Victory Monument that commemorated the heroes of the Second World War.

Sergey was on the top floor of a building that faced the street. It was an old stone building with a red-tiled roof that evoked memories that Anna had of her time in eastern Europe with Denis as they worked covert operations. It was just a building such as this that would have made an ideal location for them to set up a surveillance operation.

They reached the top of the floor and when they found Sergey's apartment Anna knocked on the door, three slow knocks, just as Alastair had instructed her. The sound of footsteps was followed by a series of locks being released in sequence until the door handle turned, and it opened revealing a man who looked many years older than his actual age probably was. Sergey stood five foot ten and had a full head of wiry grey hair that traveled in every direction. His features were faded with time and stress, all except his piercing blue eyes in which Anna saw a spark of rebellion. She knew she had never met Sergey before, but she couldn't help but think that he looked particularly familiar to her as well.

Sergey already knew it was Anna and stepped aside to let her into his apartment. As he shut the door behind Simon, he looked at Anna and raised his eyebrows toward Simon's direction.

"Alastair sent me your photo so I would know what you looked like. But who is he?" Sergey spoke English very well and with only a slight accent.

"This is Simon, my partner. Sort of," Anna introduced Simon but didn't want to get into the details of their arrangement.

Sergey looked at Simon for a while and seemed to understand that Anna was less than fond of having him in tow.

He then turned to Anna and said, "Why don't we go in the back and we can get started on what you needed me to research."

It was as if Sergey understood that Anna didn't want Simon to know about the DNA test that she needed Sergey to run. And she was thankful for his intentional vagueness.

Anna turned to face Simon as Sergey headed to the back room. "I need you to research a possible connection that Alastair had sent to me," Anna asked Simon.

"Sure, what is it?" Simon knew he wasn't welcome to join her and Sergey in the back room and he didn't seem overly bothered by it either.

"I need you to see what you can find out about a company called Quantum Security and Steve Ashbury," Anna explained.

"Ex-Senator Ashbury?" Simon asked.

"Yeah, him. Alastair found something that may connect him and that company to what is going on over here," Anna said.

"How is it connected?" Simon asked.

"Before I left, just after William brought me on, I found some bugs that were planted in my apartment. Alastair traced the shipment back to a ship that Quantum Security owned. The company was traced back to Steve Ashbury long before he was a Senator," Anna said.

"He's the Secretary of Defense right now," Simon said, he then raised his eyebrows. "You know I don't believe in coincidences."

"I know, neither do I," Anna then left Simon with the task of tracking down information on Ashbury and Quantum Security while she joined Sergey in the back room.

Anna closed the door behind her and walked over to the chair that was placed beside the desk where Sergey was sitting. He had a complete lab and computer room set up in perfect isolation in the windowless hundred square foot room they sat in. Anna could tell that it was more than a small operation, whatever Sergey was up to. She scanned the room and saw equipment that only top-level government agencies would have assembled along with a cooling system and soundproofing that enabled complete anonymity.

"Do you have the sample?" Sergey asked as he held his hand stretched out toward Anna.

"Yes," Anna answered as she reached into her bag and retrieved the skin tissue that she extracted from her nail bed after the attack in the cemetery.

Sergey held the bag up to the light on his desk and nodded, "Looks like more than enough to run a sample."

"How long do you think it would take?" Anna asked.

"Not long. Twenty minutes – top," Sergey said with a wave of his hand.

Anna nodded and sat back in the chair and looked around the room.

"Impressed?" Sergey asked. He was removing the sample from the bag and placing it in a tube to prepare the sample for DNA extraction.

"Very. How did you manage all of this?" Anna asked as she waved her arm around the room.

"Alastair," Sergey said. He was peering through a microscope at the sample he extracted.

"How do you know Alastair?" Anna asked.

"He is my son," Sergey responded nonchalantly.

He stood up and walked over to a scanner machine and placed the tube inside the miniature steel box and closed the door. He pressed a sequence of keys and once he hit 'enter' the laser buzzed to life and Sergey returned to his desk and sat in the chair next to Anna.

"You didn't know?" Sergey had noticed the surprised look on Anna's face at the mention of Alastair being Sergey's son.

"No," Anna said.

"Well, I am not surprised. Alastair is very secretive about his life. Even more so since he began working for MI6," Sergey smiled and shook his head from side to side.

"I guess I just assumed Alastair was British. His last name is Sewell," Anna said.

"He began to use his mother's last name when he was in high school. Pashkevich was a bit of a mouthful for many Brits," Sergey said with a chuckle. "He was born in England. I am British as well, I just came to it later in life." Sergey explained. "You see, the people in this region suffered much oppression at the hands of the Russians over the years. My family had drawn the unfortunate attention of the Russians just because we were Jewish. Britain offered many Jews from this area refuge during that time and after a while, I became an official citizen. I was allowed to work with the British government undercover to help expose a cell that they thought was infiltrating information back to the Russians. I jumped at the chance since it was the least I could do. My science degree offered me the perfect cover as a professor at the university."

"I had no idea. I am so sorry," Anna said.

"It was a brutal time for us, but we were lucky and made it out. It's how I can repay Britain by saving us," Sergey said.

"How about all this equipment? It must throw your power consumption out of wack from your neighbors?" Anna asked.

"Alastair took care of that as well. There are solar panels rigged and a generator that runs from the basement of the building two blocks away. I am, technically, almost off the grid," Sergey chuckled.

Just then an alarm began to buzz on Sergey's desk and Simon came running through the door.

"We have to go now, Anna," Simon was pulling his bag over his shoulder and pulling the straps tight.

Sergey was tapping the keys on his keyboard and the six CCTV cameras he monitored came into view. They could see approximately nine bodies in completely blacked-out gear making their way in commando mode toward Sergey's apartment.

"How did they find us?" Anna asked Sergey.

"I have no idea. All my equipment is rerouted to buildings at least a couple of blocks away. You must have been followed," Sergey explained.

Sergey pushed his chair back and motioned for Anna and Simon to follow him to the other side of the room.

"Go through here," and he pushed open a door on the other side of his room. "The hall will lead you to a stairwell. It's private so you will not pass anyone. Take it all the way to the bottom and then follow the tunnel. It'll take you a mile east of here. The tunnel is equipped with a transmission-blocking scanner, so you won't be able to use your phones at all in there and when you reach the end, you will arrive at a small building." Sergey placed a set of keys in the palm of Anna's hand. "Take the car that is there and make your way away from here."

"What about you, Sergey?" Anna did not like the idea of leaving him behind, especially now that she knew he was Alastair's father.

"Don't worry about me. Alastair has a contingency for a situation just like this," he then leaned in close to Anna and whispered. "I'll send the results to Alastair and he can forward them to you. Now go!"

And with that Sergey pushed Anna through the door and quickly closed it and engaged the lock.

Anna and Simon took the stairs to the bottom, jumping each flight to the landings in-between. When they reached the bottom, they ran the length of the tunnel without saying a word. But Anna knew that the same words were running through Simon's mind, 'Who is tracking us and how did they find us?'

The tunnel was damp and smelled of mold and rot from years of containment. The light was faint but still strong enough to illuminate the ground as they ran as fast as they could to reach the very end. The stone that lined the tunnel was there before the first world war. Anna shuddered at the number of people that must have tried to flee death and persecution through these same tunnels.

When they reached the end there was a small steel door that had a faint yellow light shining down on the entrance.

Simon grabbed the handle and turned it and jammed his shoulder as he tried to push it open.

"It's locked," Simon said as he turned to Anna who was standing behind him.

Anna pushed him aside and opened the palm of her hand revealing a keychain with three keys attached to the ring.

Anna fingered the keys and recognized the car key with the large black VW logo on the end and next to that one was a small key that looked like it belonged to a safe. Anna tried the last key which slipped into the lock effortlessly and she turned the handle.

They made their way into the building on the other side of the door and took the narrow stairwell up to the ground floor. Immediately to the left was the entrance to the garage. Anna yanked the door open and was pleased to see that there was a car parked inside. Simon reached to grab the door handle when Anna grabbed his shoulder and pulled him around to face her.

"Empty your bag," Anna commanded.

"What? Now! Are you serious, we need to get out of here!" Simon shouted.

"Someone followed us, which means somehow we were tracked!" Anna yelled.

"I swear to you, I'm on your side!" Simon leaned in and shouted in Anna's face. "Do you think I would be dumb enough to try and trick you twice!"

"Now! Empty your bag!" Anna yelled.

"Fine," Simon loosened the straps on his bag and swung it around in front of him. He unzipped the top and pulled out his laptop then turned his bag upside down and shook the entire contents out on the garage floor. "There!"

Anna reached into her pocket and grabbed her phone. After she unlocked the phone, she opened the scanner app she had designed to search for bugs.

She swept over the contents sprawled over the ground in front of her and over Simon's computer. She then scanned Simon from the top of his head to his feet. The scan came back clean. There was nothing on Simon or his things.

"I don't understand," Anna said. "How did they find us?"

"Check your bag now," Simon said.

"Are you serious?" Anna said.

"Look, I don't blame you for questioning me. I guess I deserve that, but you were the one who said your apartment was bugged. How do you know you weren't the one who was traced?" Simon said.

Anna knew he could be right. Anna emptied the contents of her bag and scanned them to find that they were clean. She stood up straight and started from her feet as she scanned her entire body. She ran the phone sensor over each leg and her midsection before circling her head and each arm. When the scan reached her wrist bone the scanner flashed red on her phone screen.

"It's your watch!" Simon shouted, "Take it off and give it to me."

Anna froze just staring at the watch. It was the one she grabbed from Denis's locker. It didn't make any sense.

"Anna!" Simon shouted.

Anna quickly unstrapped the wristband and handed the watch to Simon. He took it and turned it over. He pried off the back with a knife he extracted from his pocket and saw the tiny tracker that was placed inside the watch mechanism. With the tip of the blade, Simon popped the tracker loose and put it on the cement ground. He brought the force of his boot heel down upon the tracker crushing it completely. Anna ran the scanner over the tracker, and it confirmed it was dead.

Simon returned Anna's watch to her and said, "I didn't think anyone wore watches anymore?"

The two gathered the items from their packs that were scattered on the garage floor and quickly repacked them.

"I'll drive. I know a couple of back routes to get out of town," Simon held out his hand for the keys which Anna pressed into the palm of his hand. They exited the garage a short while later and were making their way down a back lane when she realized Simon was speaking to her.

"I said, I what were you doing in the room with Sergey?" Simon repeated his question.

"Oh, just trying to track some banking info," Anna lied. "How about you, any success?"

"Actually, yes," Simon said.

Anna's interest was piqued, and she turned in her seat to face Simon and waited for him to continue.

"And?" Anna prompted him.

"You're not going to like it," Simon said as he pulled out onto a road heading out of town.

CHAPTER 13-

"While you were working with Sergey one of my contacts was able to pull up some information on Quantum Security and our guy Ashbury," Simon explained as he drove. "It seems that Quantum has its dealing in all sorts of countries around the world. Hot spots actually, and I don't mean vacation spots either." Simon reached into the back seat as he continued to drive and grabbed his laptop and handed it to Anna.

"Open up the file folder I have on the desktop. It's the information my contact was able to find. It includes company filing records and most of their financials. Turns out it is a pretty successful security company. Governments routinely hire out their services for various covert operations," Simon explained.

"That's not that unusual. Government agencies often will use the services of security companies, especially in foreign countries.

"I know, but how many do you know that work in conjunction with governments that are at odds with one another?" Simon asked and then answered his own question. "Not often. Because it isn't good for repeat business."

Anna opened the file and began to scan through the countries and names of executives linked to Quantum Security. "And how long has Ashbury been connected to Quantum?"

"That's the thing. Since forever. It's his family's business," Simon explained.

"I thought the Ashbury's were an oil family from Texas?" Anna said as she proceeded to open the file marked *financials*.

"They are. They have their fingers in many pies. Picture how big you think they are and then multiply it by ten. There are so many layers of shell companies, you would have to know what you were looking for if you wanted to find it," Simon explained.

"Interesting," Anna said. "But how does it relate to our guy in Latvia and the explosion that took out our team?"

"One of the executive names on the Quantum Security roster was Joshua Collins," Simon said.

Anna turned her head quickly and faced Simon. Joshua was an agent she initially worked with when she began in William's department. Joshua was more of a mathematical genius than a field agent and he traced hidden accounts that were linked to terrorist cells and organizations. Joshua was responsible for uncovering over twenty suspicious organizations that were linked to hundreds of clean accounts. After a couple of years, Joshua claimed the stress was too much and he resigned. He opted for a quiet early retirement as an accountant back in his hometown. Or so Anna thought.

Anna opened the Quantum Security folder that Simon had downloaded to his computer and scanned the list for Joshua's name. She found it close to the bottom and ran her finger across the screen to the dates that indicated when Joshua worked for Quantum.

"It says here that Josh worked for Quantum since before he resigned with us," Anna said.

"I noticed that too. It looks like he started with them about six months before he quit our organization," Simon said.

"Our organization?" Anna snapped.

"Yes! Our organization!" Simon said. "Look, Anna, I don't know when you are going to let this go, or even if you can, but I am on your side."

Anna didn't respond to Simon's outburst. She still wasn't sure if she could trust him, but she was coming to the realization that she had less choice the longer they were on the same mission together.

"When I compared the date that Josh started with Quantum to the files he was covering when he was working for us, I found something suspicious," Simon explained.

Anna's phone buzzed inside her jacket and she ignored it, she didn't want to interrupt Simon.

"It was the same time we were tracking the cell in Iran. Remember? The Executive branch of the government was suspicious of Iran and Turkey interfering in our fuel supply. Well, it was around the same time Josh was investigating that money trail when he was probably approached by Quantum," Simon surmised.

"I remember it was one of the only times Josh wasn't able to find a financial link between the organizations involved," Anna recalled. Her phone buzzed again.

"Yeah, a little odd don't you think?" Simon said.

"Yeah, odd," Anna said.

"Then there's the matter of Quantum's holdings. They're spread out all over the world. They have garnered control over various utility companies in Russia, Syria, Turkey, Iran, and several countries in Europe – including Latvia. They're registered under different names of course and each holding is not large enough to draw any attention from the governments. But considering Quantum is in control of all the subsidiaries, they essentially hold the majority control of utilities and companies in most countries and could disable them at will."

"This could become a problem real fast," Anna said. "If they're so widespread, who would monitor their dealings?"

"They haven't done anything illegal yet. Right now, they are just a company with several holdings and subsidiaries. And Ashbury has been able to keep his name off any relevant documents, but since it's ultimately controlled by his family, I'm sure he has more than a small say in how decisions are directed. And I don't have to remind you as Secretary of Defense that could pose a huge problem globally with a number of our allies," Simon said.

Anna's phone continued to buzz, and she tried to ignore it.

"I was partway through some of Josh's emails that my contact was able to duplicate from his network when I realized we had been followed to Sergey's. I didn't get a chance to read all of them. They are in a subfolder in the Quantum file marked Collins," Simon refocused his attention on the road as Anna clicked the file open on the laptop.

"What is this file labeled 'Blackwater'?" Anna asked.

"Not sure, I wasn't able to open it," Simon said.

Anna scanned the emails and they all seemed innocuous. Family emails, college reunions, and then there was one that stood out not because of the subject line but because of the date. It was dated a week ago from a hotel confirming his reservation.

"This is interesting," Anna said as she began to read the email.

"What?" Simon asked.

"Josh is going to a wedding this week," Anna said.

"So?" Simon said.

"The wedding is for Katya Abramovich. She is Alexei Abramovich's daughter," Anna said. "And it looks like Josh is a special guest of Alexei's."

Simon and Anna looked at each other and at once she knew what he was thinking.

"Looks like we are heading to a Russian mobster's wedding," Simon announced as he swerved the car onto the shoulder before making a wide U-turn in the road. Anna's phone buzzed again and this time she reached into her pocket and pulled it out. It was Alastair. She answered the phone and held it up to her ear.

"Sorry, a bit of confusion at Sergey's," Anna said into the phone.

"I know, he told me," Alastair said.

"You didn't tell me he was your father," Anna said.

"Would it have mattered?" Alastair said.

"You know it wouldn't have mattered. It was nice to have met him. He has been through a hell of a lot," Anna said.

"Yes, he has. He has a good heart, and he is making a difference for those that want positive change. He also was able to pull a DNA sequence from the tissue sample you gave him," Alastair said.

"And?" Anna was anxious to find out who had attacked her in the cemetery in Riga.

"I need to ask you. When you were at the house and you went through the rooms is there any way the sample you had could have been contaminated?" Alastair asked.

"No, it never left my bag," Anna said.

"Are you positive?" Alastair asked.

"Alastair, what is this about? Just tell me," Anna said.

"Are you sure you didn't open it at any time?"

"Positive. What did you find out?" Anna said.

"The DNA sample that Sergey sent me came up with a match, but. ." Alastair paused.

"But what?" Anna asked.

"It was a match for Denis's DNA."

CHAPTER 14-

Anna and Simon arrived in Russia with half a day to spare before the wedding. They drove through without stopping and made it across the border at a crossing that Simon had a secret contact at.

It was getting harder and harder not to trust Simon, but Anna refused to completely let her guard down. She used her time in the car to read the research that Simon was able to get from his connection.

The financial recordings of the numerous holding companies were overwhelming at first. She could immediately see why Quantum saw Josh's skill set as very useful to their organization. He must have coordinated most of the hidden shell companies that money transferred through. Across companies and borders. And knowing what governments looked for it would have made it much easier for him to keep things hidden.

Simon and Anna made their way to a hotel across the street from the luxury hotel that Josh was staying in and that the wedding reception was being held at. As Anna was setting up her computer, Simon was breaking into the hotel's reservation system to determine what room Josh was staying in.

It didn't take Simon long to find out that Josh was in room 1216 and he quickly began to download the encryption key for his room pass onto the phone app he had designed and used many times before to access rooms of people he was tracking.

Once he was done, he closed the lid to his laptop and pulled his arms over his head, and reached them toward the ceiling. He tilted his head from side to side stretching out the muscles in his neck that grew stiff during their long ride.

Simon turned to face Anna who was sitting on the bed with her back against the wall working on her laptop. "Any ideas as to how we get into the Abramovich wedding?" Simon asked Anna.

"Just like any good spy. We initially pose as servers. I found out the company that supplies the staff for the events at the luxury hotel across the street, is also working an event at this hotel. We can grab uniforms from downstairs. Once we are inside, we can work it out from there."

"Work it out?" Simon laughed. "Well, I'll bring this along just in case." Simon held up a small vial and shook the clear liquid to show Anna its contents. "Just a drop will render anyone unconscious. For a whole night if necessary."

"Awesome," Anna raised her eyebrows and toyed with the idea of using it on Simon.

"I'm going to grab a quick shower before we go. We have a few hours before the staff starts filtering in." Simon pushed his chair back and walked into the bathroom and shut the door behind him. A few seconds later Anna heard water running and the shower spray pound against the inside of the tub.

Anna kicked her feet off the bed and placed her laptop on the night table beside where she was pretending to work on her computer.

She slipped her room key in her back pocket and with the address of her contact etched into her memory, she quietly opened the door to the room and slipped into the hallway. She knew that Simon would be out of the shower before she returned, but she would deal with explaining why she left later.

Anna replayed Alastair's words in her head most of the way on their drive to Russia. The DNA was a match for Denis. But she knew that he died in the explosion. William waited to see if anyone emerged from the building after he crawled from the rubble and Anna arrived right after the explosion. If Denis was alive, he would have been seen by one of them, and then there was the body. The first responders found Denis's body. Then there was the fact that she knew Denis better than she knew most people and they trusted each other with their lives.

She never knew Alastair to be wrong, but she just couldn't believe he was right. She was glad right now that she hadn't mentioned the skin tissue to William or Simon.

Anna had worked several undercover operations from inside Russia, and she learned to appreciate the beauty and character that was deeply rooted in the Russian people and culture. The vast collection of art, literature, and traditions was not unlike many other countries. It defined the people, and many refused to let the corruption of the Russian government or the wealthy business owners supersede what the Russian people associated as their culture.

Denis was with Anna during the covert operations in Russia and during one operation Denis was tasked with the care of a Russian operative by the name of Svetlana Kolka. She was a mid-level government worker with an extreme talent for computers, and because of her age and her physical attributes, she easily gained access to many of the top-tiered officials in both the Russian government and the companies that greatly benefited from Russian political ties.

It didn't take long for Denis to win over the affections of Svetlana, and Anna had found herself feeling jealous for the first time in her life. It wasn't Svetlana's beauty, Denis had dated many beautiful women since she knew him. It was the fact she could see in Denis's eyes that he was falling for Svetlana as quickly as she was for him.

Anna knew that Denis had kept in contact with Svetlana after they left Russia once their assignment was completed, but she never questioned him about it. Anna had hoped Svetlana hadn't moved from her apartment on Ostozhenka Street. Seeing as it was one of the most exclusive streets in the world where billionaires were known to reside, she was sure that Svetlana wouldn't have moved. That is if she was still alive.

Anna remembered the door that Denis would enter the building unnoticed and she walked around to the back where the large wooden door was still painted a bright red. Anna picked the lock and slowly opened the door and glanced inside. Once she was sure she wasn't seen, she made her way from the ground floor to the fourth-floor corner apartment where Svetlana lived. The Russian oligarch that purchased the apartment for Svetlana would visit her once a week for what Svetlana referred to as 'ego' stroking. It was important for him to feel young, admired, and adored – all the things his wife forgot about him and Svetlana easily recalled without needed prompting.

The door at the top of the staircase led to the back of the apartment where the kitchen was located. Anna was able to gain entry without being noticed again and slowly made her way through each room.

Svetlana had each room painted a bright white and all the paintings were adorned with gold-leafed frames, illuminating the artistry contained within their borders. Some were legitimately purchased, others were gifts from lovers who had obtained them illegally. Anna remembered Denis telling her that the original Blue Water Lilies painting by Monet was hanging in Svetlana's apartment and a forged copy was hanging in the Musée d'Orsay. The French museum officials were oblivious to the deception that played out right under their watch.

Anna walked gingerly into the living room and glanced at the paintings on the wall and when she spotted the familiar tones of purple and blue hanging above an extended lounge chair, she shook her head.

On the shelf next to the crystal liquor cabinet was a row of photographs. Anna noticed a photo of Denis and Svetlana on a beach, with Denis's arms wrapped around Svetlana's shoulders. It sat prominently in the center of the shelf in an antique silver frame. God how she missed Denis. She leaned in to get a closer look at the photo when she caught a flash of metal in the reflection on the glass.

She turned quickly and grabbed the gun with her left hand and as she pulled Svetlana toward her, she twisted her arm around and pried the gun from her grip. She screamed under the pressure of Anna's strength and Anna pushed her away.

"Relax, Svetlana. I'm not going to hurt you," Anna flipped the gun over in her hand and released the chamber. "The gun isn't even loaded. What were you going to do with it?" Anna tossed the gun to Svetlana who caught it with both hands.

"Who are you? Why are you in my apartment?" Svetlana was panting under the heavy pulsing of her heartbeat. Svetlana glanced at the photo that Anna was looking at and then looked back at Anna. "You're his friend, aren't you? Anna, right?" Svetlana's Russian accent was tainted with a slight inflection she picked up while studying at Oxford.

"Yeah, I didn't realize he told you about me," Anna said, surprised at the fact that Svetlana knew her name.

"We told each other a lot. We both also had a lot of secrets, but we were okay with that," Svetlana explained.

Anna refocused on why she was here, "When was the last time you saw Denis?" Anna asked Svetlana.

"Is this some kind of joke?" Svetlana snapped at Anna, "He's dead."

Svetlana turned and walked over to the long white sectional that was placed under the extended row of windows that looked down onto Ostozhenka Street. Anna walked over and sat on the opposite end of the couch.

"Why are you really here? You must also know he was killed," Svetlana asked as she pulled her sweater tight around her slim waist. Tears began to form in her eyes and as she blinked, they rolled down from her bright green eyes and landed in dark drops on her pink sweater.

"Yes. I just wanted to see what you knew," Anna explained.

"Denis and I had planned to meet in Paris. I had arranged a shopping trip and he was going to be in Europe on business. I arrived and checked into our favorite hotel and waited. When he didn't arrive, I thought he was unavoidably detained because of a case. After a couple of days, I got a little worried and tried to call him. When I couldn't get a hold of him, I had a friend who lives in New York do some digging," Svetlana wiped the tears from the corner of her eyes. "That's when he told me that there was an explosion at Denis's office and that he was dead."

"It must have been hard to find out that way, I'm sorry," Anna said, feeling the sting of losing her partner once again.

"And you? You lost your partner," Svetlana tilted her head as if to say *see, we are the same.*

"There isn't a day that goes by that I don't miss him," Anna said.

"That doesn't explain why you broke into my apartment," Svetlana folded her arms across her chest.

"Denis had told me that you have a certain skill with computers, and I need your help. I came unannounced because I couldn't have anyone know I was here," Anna explained.

Svetlana looked at Anna for a long time contemplating her decision when she finally said, "Okay, what is it you need?"

Anna breathed a silent sigh of relief and shoved her hand into her pocket and removed a jump drive.

"I have some emails and financials on this stick that I need you to help decipher," Anna held the black USB stick in her right hand waiting for Svetlana to take it.

Svetlana stood and walked over to where Anna was sitting and plucked the USB drive out of the palm of Anna's hand and motioned for her to follow into the adjoining room.

It was the only space, from what Anna could tell, that wasn't painted white. The room was lined with mahogany paneling that looked as if it had been removed from a royal library and used to renovate this space. Wires and chords were expertly placed and hidden, however, Anna had spotted three cameras that were placed in strategic locations within the room allowing complete recording from every angle.

Svetlana pulled the mouse toward her as she sat in the soft leather chair and the monitor flashed to life.

"What is it you are looking for anyway?" Svetlana asked as she inserted the drive into the computer.

"I'm trying to find a link in any of these documents to Latvia and the organization that Denis and I worked for," Anna said.

Svetlana turned to face Anna, "Does this have to do with Denis's death?"

"I'm not sure, that's what I'm trying to find out," Anna answered.

"Then you have my cooperation," Svetlana turned to face her computer and tapped at the keyboard demonstrating her advanced computer skills, and secretly wondered if Alastair would be impressed.

"Looks like several different companies with holdings in utilities around the world. They all stem back to a company in the U.S." Svetlana was talking as she was running through the document files with great speed.

"I have a computer program I developed that I can run this information through, and we can dig into some very interesting areas," Svetlana explained as she pulled up a few security boxes and entered in a series of alphanumeric codes.

Code began to scroll across the screen followed by document files that opened layering over each other on the right side of her screen.

"See," Svetlana said, marveling at her own speed.

Anna leaned in to see what she had found and was squinting to read the files as they opened on the screen.

"What did you find?" asked Anna.

"Documents from three banks in Riga that have been in service through many government changes. And some interesting deposits, they are different amounts but all made at equal intervals. It looks like over the last few years most of the transactions have been made by the same employee of the company with all the holdings."

"Joshua Collins?" Anna asked.

"Yes," Svetlana answered. "So I guess you know some information."

"Not much," Anna confessed.

"Check this out," Svetlana pointed to a graph she brought up on the screen. "I correlated the rises and falls of the stock market to the deposits. What do you see?"

"Every time there is movement from the company to buy or sell stocks, the market changes. It happens right when the transactions take place."

Anna still couldn't see how that would have anything to do with the explosion.

"Can you see if you can get into the file named 'Blackwater'?" Anna asked.

"Sure," Svetlana tapped away with her perfectly manicured fingers each time she hit enter another security box would appear and she continued to proficiently enter a different alphanumeric code pulling her deeper and deeper into the file until she had full access to the information.

"What is it?" Anna asked.

"There is an assortment of bank documents along with travel documents and passport information. It also looks like there is a list of some eastern Europeans that were being watched," Svetlana explained.

"Watched by whom?" asked Anna.

"Americans," Svetlana said. "There's a letter here sent from a University in the U.S."

"What letter?" Anna asked.

"It looks like a letter, mailed to Josh Collins. There was a scribbled note on the top before he scanned it into his file. Do you recognize the writing?" Svetlana asked.

Anna looked at the familiar handwriting and read the words slowly, 'passed to W'. "It's Josh's handwriting, I'm sure of it."

"Who is W?" Svetlana asked.

"I am not sure," Anna could only remember one person with the initial W that in their organization. William.

Anna quickly scanned the letter. It had been sent from a University in Boston. The document contained proof implicating the U.S. in a price–fixing scheme of great proportions, affecting world stock markets all to line the pockets of a couple of key government officials and one large corporation. At the center of it, was Ashbury. The document contained an elaborate system uncovered by a student writing her doctorate in economics. From the sound of the letter, it seemed as if she was on a personal basis with Josh.

"There is something else on the files. There is another person on the bank documents. Eloria Evanishyn. But she hasn't made any transactions in about seven years."

Anna didn't recognize the name but made a mental note of it.

"I'll print out the bank addresses and account information, names, and numbers," Svetlana offered.

"Can you print the letter you found as well?" Anna asked.

Svetlana nodded and keyed in the sequence to print the documents.

"Do you still have contact with Josh?" Svetlana asked.

"No, he left our organization a while ago. But I found an email containing an invite to the Abramovich wedding and I plan on being there to speak with him," Anna explained.

"I assume you know who Abramovich is?" Svetlana asked.

Anna nodded, "I'm fully aware of the scope of Abramovich's business dealings and the security he surrounds himself with."

Svetlana raised her eyebrows and said, "You're as brave as Denis said you were."

As they continued to wait for the documents to print, Anna pulled out the photograph she found in his locker and handed it to Svetlana.

"Do you recognize this at all?" Anna asked.

Svetlana took the photo from Anna and looked at it for a couple of minutes and then a slow smile began to spread across her face.

"It looks like Denis. He showed me a photo of himself when he was a little boy and it looked just like this boy," Svetlana handed the photo back to Anna.

Anna pointed to the other people in the picture, "Do you know who they may be?"

Svetlana shook her head, "Denis never spoke about his family. I think it was painful for him, so I didn't push it."

Anna looked at the picture for a while and then remembered the address on the back.

"Can you look up this address?" Anna flipped the photo over to reveal the faded number and text on the back.

"Not much to go on," Svetlana typed the information from the back of the photo into her search bar on the computer.

The two women watched as dots ran across the bottom of the screen indicating that the system was running a scan.

Then the dots stopped moving and the information appeared.

The owners of Exera iela 9, Burtnieki in Latvia, were Andris and Inga Evanishyn. The same last name as the secret account holder.

CHAPTER 15-

Anna swiped her room card over the security pass and turned the handle and entered the room. Simon was sitting on a chair with his feet perched on the end of the bed tapping away on his computer. He looked up at Anna as she walked into the room.

"You know, a little note would have been nice. Where did you go?" Simon asked.

"I had to see someone," answered Anna.

"Who?" Simon asked.

"A contact, Simon," Anna tersely responded. She was keeping as much information to herself as possible.

Simon shut the lid to his laptop and walked over to the safe. He keyed in the five-digit code they set up when they first arrived in the room and waited for the lock to release. He pulled the door open and put his laptop inside.

"I grabbed the uniforms from downstairs while you were out, yours is on the bed," Simon pointed to the freshly pressed black pantsuit that was placed on the end of the bed along with a white collared shirt that completed the server's uniform. He grabbed his clothes and went into the bathroom to change and closed the door behind him.

Once she was sure Simon wasn't coming back into the room, Anna tossed the printed pages she got from Svetlana along with her laptop and USB stick into the safe and closed the door. She glanced toward the bathroom for a moment and then punched the security code into the safe's keypad and then proceeded to initiate the sequence to change the code. Once she had reprogrammed the code, she closed the cabinet door and began to change into the uniform that was going to allow her to slip past the security of the heavily guarded Abramovich wedding.

Once she was dressed, Anna pulled out her phone and began to quickly text a message to Alastair. She asked him to dig into the files relating to the explosion. She wanted to have him review any information she could find on the bodies found at the scene. She hit enter and slipped the phone back into her pocket.

As if on cue, Simon emerged from the bathroom in the server's uniform and walked over to the dresser, and picked up a set of glasses. Once he placed them on his face, he erased any signs of his rugged appearance and fit into the role of a server for the Abramovich wedding across the street.

Anna pulled her hair back into a tight ponytail and slipped a wig over her head concealing her dark brown hair and replacing her look with a cropped black hairstyle. Both Anna and Simon had to admit that the transformation was more than impressive. They couldn't risk Josh recognizing them before they were ready to confront him.

Simon handed Anna the earbud communication device along with a small pin that she placed on her collar.

"We can use these to communicate with each other at the reception," Simon explained as he slipped the miniature device in his left ear.

Simon slowly opened the hotel door and listened for any movement in the hall. When he was sure the way was clear, they slipped out of the room and made their way into the stairwell at the end of the hall. Once they reached the ground floor they emerged into the back alley and made their way around delivery trucks and linen baskets until they were on the other side of the building next to the hotel.

The two crossed the street in their disguises and sprinted down the lane toward the staff entrance at the back of the hotel.

Simon pulled Anna behind a parked truck when they heard two women who were taking a smoke break by the huge grey steel secured door. Anna and Simon crouched in wait as the workers took the last drag of their cigarettes and reluctantly began to head back into the hotel to return to work. The first woman swiped her security pass over the flat black pad mounted on the wall next to the door handle, and the second woman stepped into the building behind her and the huge steel door began its slow close on the hydraulic hinge.

Simon bolted toward the door and grabbed the handle just as the door was within an inch of closing – giving them the private access they needed. They waited a couple of seconds before pulling the door open and slipping inside.

Once they were inside, they were overwhelmed with the aroma of cooking emanating from the kitchen and Anna felt the grumbling rise in her stomach making her realize she had not eaten a solid meal in a few days. Staff was moving through the hall, and everyone seemed to be heading in different directions. Anna assumed their arrival must also have coordinated with a shift change that was taking place with the hotel staff, which was an ideal way to remain unnoticed.

Just then a woman in her fifties stepped in front of them and began to pepper them in Russian as she frantically waved her arms around in the air and pointed in the direction of the kitchen.

Simon's Russian was more up-to-date than Anna's and she was grateful when he began to explain to the woman that they were replacements for two regulars that were sick that day.

The woman shoved her fists into her hips and sighed as she shook her head and then quickly grabbed each of their arms and pulled them toward the kitchen. She pushed them in ahead of her and instructed them to listen while she went to find trays for them.

What hotel guests didn't see was the preparation leading up to the elaborate events that took place at luxury hotels such as this. Behind the scenes, the staff was not unlike other staff at other hotels. A group of servers had congregated around the kitchen manager who was explaining the evening's schedule and explaining the ingredients in the elaborate appetizers that were sure to prompt guest's queries throughout the evening. None of the information that Anna had planned on needing anyway.

The kitchen manager had nodded, indicating that he had finished his instructions for the evening which prompted the servers to scurry around and collect their trays and walked over to the counter that was lined with Rosenthal champagne glasses filled with Armand de Brignac champagne, proving that expense was no issue at this gathering.

Anna and Simon were the last to collect their glasses, choosing to hang behind the other servers. Simon removed the vial from the inside pocket of his jacket and shielded his arms behind Anna's body. He twisted the cap and poured the contents into two glasses and then replaced the vial in his jacket pocket. He placed the two glasses on Anna's tray along with five other glasses.

"The two glasses with the serum are sitting over the hotel emblem on the tray," Simon informed her as he gathered glasses for his own tray.

Once they were loaded up, they made their way into the main reception area and walked around the guests offering champagne. Anna was careful not to offer the spiked glasses to anyone not fitting their size description. It was important for them to find two guests that were the same size as she and Simon, all while searching for Josh.

"I haven't spotted him yet," Simon's voice came through the earbud in Anna's left ear. "Any luck finding two guests our size?"

"I did spot a couple who fit our sizes, however, they're in deep conversation with Abramovich so I don't think they'll be as easy to divert from the crowd," Anna spoke into the pin on her collar.

"Keep looking," Simon answered.

Anna walked through the crowd watching the throngs of couples entranced by the elaborate decorations, eight-tiered cake, and an illuminated dance floor. Anna almost had offered one of the spiked glasses to a seventy-year-old woman before she swiveled the tray and offered a glass, she knew was safe.

Just then she spotted a couple that not only shared Anna and Simon's physical attributes, but they were also standing away from the crowd, ostensibly a sympathy invite that had not connected with most of Abramovich's inner circle.

"Found two," Anna announced into her shirt pin.

She walked over to the two guests as they were admiring the elaborate floral arrangements and offered them each a glass of the spiked Armand de Brignac. In her best Russian she informed the couple that Abramovich had invited them to a private gathering in the executive suite.

The couple was so impressed with being recognized they didn't hesitate for a moment once Anna had given them directions to the room at the end of the hall.

Anna led them down the long hallway that was decorated with velvet wallpaper and gold-leafed framed paintings of Russian czars. When they reached the suite, Anna instructed them to wait inside until Mr. Abramovich could join them.

The two entered the suite and Anna closed the door behind them. She informed Simon, who was still serving drinks in the main reception, that a couple was in the room waiting. He handed the last glass of champagne to a guest who had just entered the reception hall and placed his tray on the servers filling station and began to make his way down the hall and stood beside Anna just outside the door.

The two stood quietly watching for movement in the hall and finally a couple of minutes later they heard a thud and Simon placed his hand on the door handle preparing to enter. Anna put her hand on top of Simon's and raised a finger from her other hand to her lips.

They waited a few seconds more for the second thud and then Anna smiled and nodded, "Now it's clear."

They slipped into the room and found the two unconscious guests on the floor. Anna and Simon quickly undressed the unconscious couple and placed them on the extended lounge sofa next to each other. Anna grabbed a tablecloth from the banquet table next to the wall and lay it over the couple as their bodies leaned against each other on the red velvet lounge. They dressed in the unsuspecting couple's clothes and Anna emptied the contents of the woman's purse on the table and slipped her phone inside, and with their server's clothes tossed in the closet, they made their way out of the room and toward the wedding reception.

They walked past a server holding a tray of champagne glasses and Simon took two and handed one to Anna.

Anna tilted her head, "Really?"

"What? We have to look the part," Simon smiled as he took a sip and placed his hand on the lower part of Anna's back.

"Does that fancy phone of yours that Alastair built for you still have the ability to send texts to nearby phones without having the number?" Simon asked.

Anna nodded.

"Good, get a text ready to send to Josh once we find him," Simon said.

The two made their way around the wedding reception playing the role of invited wedding guests. As they mingled closely amongst family members and business associates that the guest's list consisted of, they scanned each person for anyone resembling Josh Collins.

"He is on the other side of the room," Simon announced almost twenty minutes after they shed their serving persona.

Anna slowly twisted her head until her chin hovered over her right shoulder and glanced sideways until she spotted Josh standing in the middle of a group of men. There were five in total and judging by their security detail they were most likely business associates of Abramovich's.

Anna opened the black velvet side purse and without removing the phone she entered a text into the phone and queued it up in the app and then she walked next to Josh.

After she pressed the button to initialize the send feature, she held the phone behind her back, almost touching the edge of Josh's jacket.

When she felt the vibration of her phone, she knew the message had been sent, she had just hoped it was to Josh's phone and not one of the other men standing next to him.

Simon watched as Josh reached into his pocket and extracted his phone and read the text. The color on his face faded and he excused himself from the group of men and the conversation they were having.

Simon leaned in to whisper into Anna's ear, "Bingo, it worked."

Josh dashed out of the room and frantically made his way out into the lobby just as Anna and Simon caught up to him. Anna walked up behind Josh and grabbed his arm by the crux of his elbow and pulled him back so she could speak into his ear so only he could hear.

"Maybe we can go somewhere a little more private to talk?" Anna whispered.

Josh turned and faced Anna who had a tight grip on his arm, and it was obvious she had no intention of releasing her hold. Josh looked up at Simon who was standing behind her and, realizing he couldn't run, nodded toward the restaurant on the left.

They walked toward the restaurant and pulled open the doors and entered the vacant room, which had been closed for security precautions. Once inside Anna released Josh's arm as Simon stood next to him, leaving Josh right in the middle of their glares.

"Anna, what are you and Simon doing here? Was it you that sent that text?" Josh asked suddenly realizing the setup.

Anna nodded, "I guess the question is what are you doing here?"

"You don't understand," Josh said. "You really shouldn't be here."

"Then explain it to us," Simon responded as he crossed his arms over his broad chest.

Josh swallowed and turned to face Anna, "I don't think you understand who Abramovich is, and how important he is."

Anna tilted her head to the side, "Oh, we know who Abramovich is. The question is why would an ex-government agent, who left the bureau for a quieter line of work, be at a wedding associated with Abramovich?"

"I can't explain. Not right now," Josh said.

"Give it a try," Simon said.

"We know you're working for Quantum Security and that Ashbury's family owns it," Anna said.

Josh fixed his gaze on Anna and asked, "How did you know that?"

"How deep are you Josh? Do you even know what these guys are capable of?" Anna asked.

"You have no idea," Josh responded, and Anna could see beads of sweat forming on his forehead. "It's not what you think."

"Well, I think you were offered a bigger piece of the pie and got tired of the government wage you were pulling down with no exciting operations in the field," Simon said.

"I never wanted to be in the field, you guys know that. We were in training together," Josh explained.

"Then why did you hook up with Ashbury?" Anna asked, "I thought you left for a quieter lifestyle. I wouldn't exactly call attending social events held by the Abramovich's a quieter lifestyle."

"That's not what this is about," Josh explained.

Anna said, "Then explain it to me, Josh, because I really would like to know. Because I have been spied on, shot at, and don't forget the issue of the explosion at our office, and I can't help but think they are all connected."

Suddenly, the door flew open behind them and two large security guards rushed toward them. Just before one of them grabbed Anna, she smashed the bottom of her foot into his knee and he fell to the ground in pain.

Simon shoved Josh behind him and shielded him with his body as the second thug lunged at him with the full force of his fist. Simon leaned back but his fist landed on the edge of his jaw. Simon stumbled back into a table, grabbing the guard just before he fell.

The top of the table collapsed with a loud crack as Simon and his attacker collapsed on the ground. Simon raised his left arm and brought it down with full force on his attacker's back. The guard flipped his body over and snapped his legs in the air and righted his body and turned to face Simon who was laying on the ground below him.

The guard lifted a chair above his head and started to throw it at Simon when Anna kicked him from behind, knocking him over.

Simon sprang to his feet and nodded at Anna, "Thanks." He then reached down and grabbed the attacker's right arm and pulled it behind his back wrenching it up to the base of his neck as he pushed the force of his knee into the center of his back.

"Look out!" Josh screamed causing Anna to turn quickly just as the first attacker was hobbling to his feet, this time holding a gun in his right hand.

Anna pivoted on her right foot and landed a left roundhouse on the side of the attacker's head. He stumbled back a few steps but didn't fall to the floor. He raised his gun level with Anna's head and pulled the trigger. She dove behind one of the fallen tables for cover, just as the bullet left the gun. She rolled a couple of feet and drew the gun from inside the leg holster that was strapped to her thigh. She peered over the table and aimed a shot at the attacker, landing a bullet in the top of his thigh.

He hesitated only for a moment before continuing to fire and as he caught Simon moving out of the corner of his eye, he turned the gun in his direction firing at Simon's head. Simon pulled the thug he had in his grip in front of him and used his large girth to block the bullets. The man's body convulsed with each shot that landed on his body.

As the gunman was focused on aiming at Simon, Anna pointed her gun at him and her shot landed perfectly in the center of his forehead, ceasing his attack on Simon.

When the shots had ended, Anna and Simon slowly stood to survey the damage as well as the two dead guards.

"Josh, we need to get out of here," Anna said.

She turned to see Josh standing behind where Simon was gripping the center of his bloodstained shirt with both of his hands. His face had already begun to pale and the only noise coming from Josh's mouth were gasps for air.

"Josh!" Anna yelled as she and Simon ran toward where he was standing.

They reached him as he began to fall to his knees and Simon steadied him and gently lowered him to the ground.

"Hang on Josh, we can get you some help," Anna promised.

"I didn't do it, Anna," Josh struggled to get the words out.

"Save your strength Josh," Anna said as she was applying pressure to Josh's wounds.

"No, I need to explain, in case I don't make it," Josh muttered.

"Josh, it can wait?" Anna asked.

"No. I don't want to die with you thinking I was a traitor. I need you to know so that you'll continue searching with the information that I've found," Josh pulled Anna closer with his bloodied hand, so he could be sure she would hear him.

"I never left to work for Quantum. Not exactly. I've been working with William since before the explosion. We knew there was a possible leak, we just didn't know how bad it was or how violent it would get," Josh explained.

"You're working for William?" Anna wondered how many people William brought together in secret.

Josh nodded, "I received an envelope from my girlfriend, Sonja, who was studying for her graduate degree."

Anna remembered the scanned document from Josh's files with 'W' on the top.

"She had stumbled across information, they were patterns she noticed when she was researching her economics paper. Sonja was smart and she knew the patterns meant something and that related to what I was doing at the agency. She tried to call me, but our line was disconnected. She was working late at the university and she had found evidence that proved that there was a conspiracy that involved price-fixing for the world markets. Quantum was involved, but it also pointed toward the Russians, Latvians, and even our own government," Josh began to cough up some blood as he struggled to get his story across.

"Then what happened?" Anna pressed sensing Josh didn't have much time.

"Sonja was killed that night in the parking lot at the University. The police said it was a carjacking gone wrong, but a week later I received an envelope with copies of the documents she came across. Once I showed them to William, he agreed they warranted some digging. Sonja died because she tried to get the information to me. I owed it to her to follow the trail. So, we decided that the best thing for me to do was to go undercover with Quantum as a numbers guy, moving their banking around and helping them shield it from the government, but I was really pulling information and forwarding it to William. Then I came across a document that could have easily been missed that leads to three main accomplices. The key to moving the plan forward now."

"Then if you found out who was responsible, why are you still undercover?" Anna asked.

"I still needed more proof, but," Josh paused as he gasped for air.

"Then what?" Anna prompted Josh to continue.

"The explosion happened, and William went silent for a while. I knew we couldn't proceed without more evidence. William contacted me a short while after the explosion to let me know he was alive. We had to be careful. We had to make sure we knew without a doubt everyone who was involved," Josh gasped for air as his lungs wheezed.

"Did the leak come from our department Josh?" Anna asked.

Josh nodded, "It is more than that, this operation goes back a couple of decades. This is personal too, and so much more complicated than you think."

"What do you mean?" Simon asked.

"I followed the trail to Russia and I was able to connect them. It was a long shot, but it paid off, but I still haven't told William. One of the three worked in our department," Josh faded in and out of consciousness.

Anna shook Josh until his eyes struggled to open.

"Josh, what is Blackwater? I found a file titled Blackwater. How does it relate?" Anna asked.

"Blackwater is how I found the leak. I almost missed it," Josh's head fell back, and he gasped for air.

"Where is Blackwater?" Anna shook Josh until he lifted his head and took in a big gulp of air.

"It's not where, but who," Josh said.

"Who Josh, who was it?" Anna pleaded.

Josh strained to get out one last sentence, "Just follow the money," then Josh muttered a name that neither Simon nor Anna understood, and his body went limp as he took his final breath.

CHAPTER 16 –

Anna and Simon slipped out the back exit of the restaurant before Abramovich's security team began to pile into the restaurant. They were in the back lane of their hotel across the street as half a dozen security men were assessing the carnage left behind in the struggle inside the restaurant.

Anna and Simon slipped into their hotel and moved along the hallway unnoticed, partially because the evening staff was more interested in the football game on the television than any guests that may have been wandering the halls.

They rode up the elevator in silence both feeling confused and frustrated with the little information that Josh was able to share before he died.

Simon was the first to speak, "Did you have any idea William had someone else on this operation?"

"I didn't even know you were in until I was at the safehouse. And even then, I wonder if William would have told me if I hadn't run into you," Anna snapped.

The elevator ding alerted Anna and Simon that they had reached their floor and as it glided to a smooth stop the doors quietly slid open. Anna stepped out of the elevator hoping it would be vacant as she glanced over at Simon's bloodied white shirt and her dress that was stained with Josh's blood.

She was sure if someone had seen them that they would have attracted the attention of the police or security. Neither of which was of interest to Anna nor Simon.

Simon reached into the inside pocket of his jacket and pulled out the room pass key as they neared their room. The sound of sliding drawers and a closet being slammed shut came from the other side of their hotel room door. Simon quickly passed the room key over the black security pad and the light went from red to green followed by a click indicating the lock had been released.

Simon turned the handle and pushed the door open into the room and suddenly stopped with the force of the door latch that was flipped over from inside the room. Simon smashed the weight of his shoulder into the door repeatedly until on the fourth time, the screws holding the latch in place finally loosened from the frame.

Simon fell into the room stumbling his first couple of steps and then regaining his balance he made his way to the open window at the opposite end of the room.

The drapes fluttered with the wind that blew in through the open window and when Simon finally reached the window, he peered through to see two men getting into a black sedan that was waiting below.

"Damn it!" Simon exclaimed. "That latch gave them just enough time to make it down."

Simon turned and faced the mess strewn about the room.

Anna saw the contents of their bags emptied onto the floor of the room. Neither of them had many pieces of clothing, but whoever was in this room made a good attempt at removing each item as they searched for whatever they were sent to find.

"What are the chances any fingerprints were left?" Simon asked in jest.

"None," Anna responded.

Simon pulled open the cabinet door revealing the room safe. The edge of the door had gashes on the side indicating that someone had tried to pry open the safe during their search.

"Looks like we interrupted our guests before they had a chance to get into the safe," Simon said.

Simon keyed the code into the safe and pressed the enter key but the code flashed red. He tried a second time, this time Anna caught sight of what he was doing, and she remembered she had changed the code when she put her computer and jump drive inside.

When the safe keypad flashed red again Simon slammed his fist against the side of the cabinet in frustration.

"Here, let me," Anna said as she reached over Simon's shoulder and entered a different code into the keypad and pressed the enter key, not worrying about shielding the code from Simon. The door popped open revealing the contents were still safely located inside.

"You want to tell me why you changed the code without telling me?" Simon asked.

Anna opened the door to the safe and pulled out her laptop, the USB stick, and the papers that Svetlana had printed for her that afternoon. She tossed them on the bed and sat down beside the pile.

"I still wasn't sure that I could trust you," Anna explained.

"How are we going to work together Anna if you don't learn to trust me?" Simon snapped.

"I went to visit an old contact of Denis's today. She has unique computer skills and was able to extract more information from Josh's files you accessed," Anna grabbed the printed sheets and handed them to Simon.

Simon sat on the second bed and grabbed the paper from Anna and began to flip through the various sheets that indicated bank accounts and transfers.

"There are three main banks that keep showing up and the transactions all coincide with major changes in the market," Anna explained.

"How major?" Simon asked as he flipped through the sheets.

"Billions of dollars," Anna said. "And the accounts are all held by governments, not corporations."

"And they are governments that aren't necessarily allies. It doesn't make sense," Simon said as he tossed the papers on the bed.

"It's most likely, the governments are funding their wars and military attacks by manipulating the markets," Anna explained.

"But why work together on this and risk being outed?" Simon asked.

"Because it only works on a scale this big if both sides are involved. They each have equal amounts to lose, so one government can't reveal the other's involvement without losing out themselves," Anna said.

"So, government disagreements and fighting over policies, is that all for appearances?" Simon asked.

"It's politics Simon, it's about votes and how well you can fool the public voters. Let them think they know what they are getting but really it is about keeping the machine working behind the scenes," Anna said then added. "Don't ask me to explain how the government works."

"So, how are Ashbury and Quantum involved?" Simon asked.

"They're the smokescreen. The shield. They have the bodies that move the money and that keeps the government's fingers out of the mess. They seem to be the agents for everyone," Anna said. "And with Ashbury connected to the current administration, he has the perfect avenue for any inside information."

Simon leaned back and rested the weight of his body on his arms, "So what else do I need to know?"

"You know that when William first brought me in, he had me track an agent from the Special Activities Division, Logan James," Anna said, and Simon nodded.

"Well, I followed him to Latvia, where he was killed, and I was attacked. But before he was killed, he met with a Dr. Petrov. Not sure what type of doctor, but Logan had paid him for a vial containing an amber liquid."

"Were you able to get it?" Simon asked.

"No," Anna explained. "The meeting was interrupted, and Dr. Petrov was killed. Logan fled with the vial and I chased him into a cemetery. I had Logan cornered and was just about to get the vial when I was knocked out. The attacker got the vial and killed Logan."

"So, we still don't know very much," Simon said.

"Not really," Anna said. "There are two things. One, my apartment was bugged when I returned from Washington when I first tracked Logan. The bugs were traced back to a shipment of devices that was recorded by our government had lost. Alastair was able to find out that they were from a ship called The Seaforth. It was a Russian trolling ship that was found in Swedish waters and the cargo was confiscated by the U.S. government."

"How does all of this connect?" Simon asked.

"The Seaforth was owned by Quantum Security, Ashbury's family company. Two of the U.S. officers that were among the crew that confiscated the cargo were William Lewis and Juris Ledin, my father," Anna explained.

Simon stared at Anna not sure what to say next, "Did you tell William you knew?"

"No, Alastair just confirmed it for me," Anna said.

"So, let me get this straight. Russia and the U.S. are primarily rigging the market flow of goods to control the prices. They release and hold goods to force a fluctuation in the market price and invest accordingly," Simon said.

Anna nodded, and Simon continued, "Then Quantum has been involved for several decades as the financial middlemen also doubling as government security being able to move documents, information, and people making sure the trail is never revealed."

"Essentially, yes," Anna said.

"Then why the explosion?" Simon asked.

"The leak that Josh said they found worked inside our division. I suspect it was either a rogue agent on their part that was breaking out or just a faction that was getting in their way. Either way, it was meant to shut us down. William and Josh must have been getting too close to the truth," Anna surmised.

"But what I don't get," Anna continued. "Is why Quantum just didn't have the person responsible for the leak killed. Why take out a huge division and risk drawing attention?"

"Because Quantum didn't know who it was," Simon said. "Think about it. It couldn't have been one of their guys."

"It must have been an outside threat to their operation," Anna added.

"And what is Blackwater?" Simon asked.

"I don't know. Josh was about to tell me before he died. I couldn't make out the name he said. His voice was too weak," Anna was frustrated at the circles they seemed to be running in.

"He said he almost missed it. Maybe it isn't related to Quantum. At least not directly," Simon guessed.

"Makes sense. So, we could be dealing with two operations then," Anna said.

"Possibly," Simon said, "But you mentioned a couple of things. What was the other?"

"When I was attacked in the cemetery, I managed to see something before I was knocked out," Anna explained.

"What was that?" Simon leaned forward.

Anna pulled up her sleeve, "This tattoo."

CHAPTER 17-

"That's a very specific tattoo Anna, are you sure?" Simon said.

"Positive," Anna rubbed her forehead with her hand, "That's why I checked your arm when I found you at the safehouse. I wasn't sure I could trust you, you know, after what happened."

Simon nodded, "And now?"

"Now I'm still not sure what to think, but I'm pretty sure after the last few days that I can at least trust you," Anna laughed. "You may be the only person I can trust right now, besides Alastair."

"So, what do we do now?" Simon said. "It seems like our trail gets cold as soon as we get any information. If we can't trust William, what now?"

"I'm not sure I can't trust William, I'm just not sure if he is telling me everything," Anna said.

"Isn't that the same thing?" Simon said.

"Not really," Anna pulled out the paper with the banking information she received from Svetlana.

"This has the addresses and the banking information from the three key banks in Latvia where the transactions have been made, I think we should follow up on them," Anna handed the paper to Simon.

"Unless your contact can get us more information on these, I think we need to go to Latvia and check these out for ourselves," Simon said.

"I agree, but I'm not even sure what we're looking for," Anna said. "I think that we need to find out who Eloria Evanishyn is."

"Who is that?" Simon asked.

"Not sure how she is connected, but she had been making regular deposits until about seven years ago. Then they just stopped. If we can find her, maybe we can get some answers," Anna suggested.

"If she's still alive," Simon added.

"Let's hope she is. Right now, she is our best hope for finding a connection," Anna looked down at her dress and then at the clothes thrown around the floor. "We should maybe change and get out of here."

"Agreed," Simon gathered some of his clothes from the floor and made his way into the bathroom, "I'll give you some time to get changed."

Anna grabbed Simon's hand as he walked past her, "Thanks for today Simon. I haven't exactly made it easy for you, but you've been like a partner since we met at the safehouse."

Simon leaned down until his face was a couple of inches from Anna's and said, "That's because I am your partner, Anna."

They stayed in that awkward position for a couple more seconds before Anna released Simon's arm and he then straightened up and went into the bathroom to change.

Anna quickly changed out of the blood-stained gown and found her jeans and a top in the pile of clothes on the floor. She was just about finished packing when Simon emerged from the bathroom looking like she had remembered him, but this time without the harsh edge she had viewed him with previously.

They gathered their passports and gear and left the hotel room, knowing it was just a matter of time before the crew here earlier returned to finish their search. Anna grabbed their bloodstained clothes and wrapped them in a sheet from the bed and tossed the bundled items into the laundry cart as they passed a room attendant on the way to the stairs.

They were exiting the hotel garage park as police were directing traffic along the street. They were searching each car for suspects from the commotion in the hotel across the street. Simon pulled the car out into the road and cursed under his breath as he was waved into a line of cars heading toward a check stop situated between the two hotels. As the car came to a stop a Russian officer approached the car and instructed Simon to lower his window.

The officer leaned down to the open window and instructed, "Pozhaluysta, udostover'tes'."

Simon responded with a thick British accent, "I'm sorry officer, I don't speak Russian."

"Identification, please," the officer repeated without a change in his facial expression or tone.

Simon nodded and removed a U.K. passport from his jacket pocket. Anna did the same and reached across Simon and placed it in the officer's outstretched hand.

The Russian officer flipped open both passports to the photos and leaned in to compare them to Simon and Anna. He then unfolded a sheet with photos taken from the security cameras inside the Abramovich wedding reception and took another look to compare the two individuals on the page to the two sitting in the car.

Anna could see the image of her and Simon walking with Josh to the restaurant. Anna's short-cropped wig and Simon's glasses and slicked-back hair were just enough to fool the Russian officer.

He folded the passports shut and handed them both to Simon. And with a thick Russian accent, he said, "You're free to go Mr. Pembroke." And he waved them ahead as he approached the next car to inspect their identification.

Anna smiled as she and Simon made their way through the maze of security checks and toward the Latvian border.

For the first time since she arrived in Europe, Anna felt like she could truly fall into a deep sleep, trusting that Simon was on her side. When she awoke, she realized they were on the outskirts of Riga.

"Why did you let me sleep so long, Simon?" Anna asked as she wiped her eyes clear. "I could've helped with driving."

"You seemed like you needed the rest," Simon smiled at Anna and she could feel she was warming to him again. "I got you a coffee and something to eat when I last stopped for fuel."

Anna noticed the rich smell of coffee had filled the interior of the car. She pulled a cup from the drink holder and took a long sip and felt it warm her as she swallowed. "Thank you, Simon."

Simon responded with a smile.

Anna unwrapped the brown paper bag and pulled out the toasted bagel inside. She had devoured it before she had a chance to finish her coffee and leaned back in her seat.

"I think we should go right to the bank that Eloria had been making deposits at, we need to find a way to track her down," Anna suggested.

Simon laughed, "We're about five minutes from that one now. I was thinking the same thing."

They arrived at the bank and Simon found a spot to park directly across the street.

"How is your Latvian?" Simon asked Anna.

"Pretty good. How's yours?" Anna asked Simon.

"Passible. Why don't you take the lead?" Simon suggested.

Anna smiled as she walked up the steps with Simon at her side. She approached the woman sitting behind the desk, she was in her early twenties and possibly more easily fooled. As soon as the young woman looked at Simon her eyes were transfixed on his rugged looks and his perfectly sculpted upper body. Her attraction to Simon along with her assumed inexperience her an easy target.

Anna launched into Latvian with her story of an aunt that passed away the previous month. As Anna wiped fake tears from the corner of her eye, she introduced Simon as her brother and said that they were trying to find a relative who was from this area about an estate they needed to settle.

Anna told the young blonde girl that they didn't have much information to go on except her cousin's name and the fact that she banked here about seven years ago.

Just as the girl began to hesitate, Anna told her it was important because Simon was going to take over the estate and move here to help run the family business. Anna happened to let it slip that Simon was single and had nobody but their cousin to rely upon.

The young blonde who was quickly enamored with Simon jumped at the opportunity to make a good impression with him and tapped away at her keyboard and after a few minutes was able to find the file Anna was looking for.

She printed out a sheet with all the contact information on it. At the top was a photo taken seven years ago, as per bank policy for all their account holders. As she folded the sheet and passed it to Simon, she said she shouldn't have done this, but she could tell they needed the help.

She handed the sheet to Simon and as he was about to take it, she held it back and grabbed a pen from next to her computer. She scribbled her name and number on the back and said he could contact her if he needed any help finding his way around town.

Simon winked and promised to contact her as soon as he was settled. He reached over with his right hand and held her hand gently as he drew her gaze toward his eyes and said he was looking forward to seeing her soon. While his left hand slipped behind the computer that was directly in front of her and he attached the miniature router to the base of the monitor that would allow him to hack into the bank's system from within five hundred meters away.

Anna and Simon walked out of the bank and left the blushing receptionist behind.

They exited the bank and turned right and walked toward the café that was next to the bank. Simon walked directly to the table that was against the wall while Anna ordered a couple of coffees and picked a couple of sandwiches from behind the glass-encased window.

Anna returned with two hot mugs of coffee and two warmed sandwiches that were laden with aromatic cheese. Anna could feel the hunger rise in her stomach as she carried the tray the distance to the table where Simon sat.

"Great idea, I'm starving!" Simon grabbed a sandwich and stole a bite and rolled back his eyes as the tastes landed on his palate.

Anna didn't bother holding back and found her way through half of the sandwich before she lowered it to take a sip of her coffee. She wiped the melted cheese from the corner of her mouth and asked Simon, "So what is it you were doing in there."

Simon smiled, "You're not the only one with a friend with toys. I placed a specialized miniature router on the back of the receptionist's computer so I could look inside the bank's computer system."

"And your little flirting episode with the receptionist?" Anna asked as she lifted the warm crusty bun to her mouth.

"I had to distract her somehow. Why? You're not jealous, are you?" Simon asked with a crooked smile.

"Ha! You wish," Anna stammered through a full mouth as she let herself laugh for a momentary break from the stress of the last few days. It made her think of when she worked alongside Denis. It was always so easy to work with him, but she shook the memory out of her head and took a sip of coffee and washed down the last bite of the sandwich.

"Okay, check this out," Simon said as he motioned for her to sit beside him so she could see the screen. With their backs to the wall, Anna watched as Simon opened file after file with such speed that Anna almost had trouble following what he was doing.

"Are those security video files?" Anna asked.

"Yeah. The bank keeps them on file for several years. Pull up some of the transaction dates on the bank statement."

Anna flipped through the file and read out the first three dates from the top of the list.

"Too far back," Simon said as he tapped away at the computer keyboard. "Try at least six months later."

Anna read out three more dates and watches as three video files opened along the bottom of Simon's computer screen.

Anna and Simon leaned in as he played the first video file. Simon speed through the video until the time stamp was ten minutes before when the bank transaction was registered. And they watched the screen. For a small bank, there was a surprisingly large number of people coming and going and making transactions.

"There," Anna pointed to the screen where the video captured a man walking into the bank. The man's face was shielded with a hat and the angle of the camera was pointed more toward the tellers, filming most of the bank's patrons on a sideways angle. He walked toward an open teller and handed her a paper and an envelope of cash.

Simon looked at the time stamp on the bank transaction, "It matches the time stamp."

The man tapped his right hand on the top of the counter as the teller processed the deposit. They watched as the teller counted the money, stamped the deposit slip, and tapped a sequence of keys into her keyboard. Once she was done, she looked up at the man and returned his stamped record to him.

He turned to leave, and the camera momentarily caught his face before he lowered the brim of his hat, once again shielding his face from view.

"Go back, go back," Anna instructed.

Simon rewound the tape to the moment where the teller handed him the deposit slip and as the man turned around, Simon paused the film. As the man's face was fully visible Simon expanded the screen and they could clearly identify the man.

"That's Logan. Logan James. The man I followed to Riga and who was killed," Anna confirmed. "Ok. So, we now know for sure that he was involved."

Simon played the next video. They easily found the moment in the video when the recorded deposit was made and once again, they were able to identify that it was Logan at the bank.

Simon opened the third video and once again located the position in the video film where the recorded deposit was made. Again, they were able to identify that it was Logan. The bank was a little busier and some lines formed at each teller's station. The one that Logan stood in was no exception. Behind Logan stood four people waiting patiently to each reach the teller. Once Logan had folded the stamped transaction record into his pocket he turned and began to walk toward the exit of the bank.

"What's that?" Anna said as they watched the last man in line turn as Logan walked past him and he began to follow Logan out of the bank.

Simon reversed the video and they watched again as the man purposefully kept his face from the camera and he looked down toward his feet. When Logan walked by him, the man turned to follow without hesitation or lifting his face.

He walked the same path that Logan did and left the bank through the same door. Never once lifting his face toward the camera.

"Any idea who that might be?" Simon asked Anna.

Anna watched as Simon replayed the video. She couldn't put her finger on it, but she thought that something seemed familiar. She dismissed her concerns as a side effect of her lack of sleep and time out of the field. "No, I can't see his face clearly. At least I'm sure it's a man."

Simon continued to scan the records for any more video recordings that they could view and decided to attempt to run a motion-recognition software on the image of the man from the bank. It was a trial software that one of his dark-room contacts designed and Simon wasn't completely sure that it wasn't being used to gather information on people while agents used it to scan suspects.

Anna returned her attention to the bank reports that itemized the dates and amounts of the deposits made at the bank.

"Don't you think these are odd amounts to be depositing?" Anna asked Simon as she pointed to a few lines in the banking document.

"Maybe it's meant to throw the banking regulators off any trail," Simon suggested.

"Maybe," Anna continued to scan the document. There was something she was missing. She could feel it.

Simon noticed the intense look on her face as she scanned the document.

"What is it Anna?" he asked, now drawn into the banking document himself.

"All the deposits are made to the same four bank accounts. Also, each time there are three separate deposits. And look, the numbers are structured very differently from the other bank numbers in the files," Anna pointed out to Simon.

"Well, it is an old European bank. Maybe the bank had just changed their numbering system over the years," Simon suggested, but not convincingly. Anna could tell he also thought it was a little peculiar.

"No, the banking regulations are too tight," Anna explained. "Then there are the deposit amounts. Look at this one, $219, $1500, and $5,569. Odd amounts for what may be a global conspiracy involving a company as large as Quantum Security, don't you think?"

Simon nodded, he had to agree with Anna. Everything was just odd enough to be out of place but not large enough to attract attention.

"Then if the amounts are not large enough to fund anything of large importance maybe they are a code," Simon suggested.

"Exactly what I was leaning toward," Anna worked hard to not let the excitement show in her voice. She didn't want to attract any unwanted attention from fellow patrons of the café.

"And remember what Josh said right before he died," Simon said.

"Yeah, he said to follow the money. He was trying to tell us that there is a code in the deposits. It has to be," Anna said.

"Each time there is a deposit made to the banks it is one of the four accounts. And as you have stated, the account numbers are a little odd." Simon said.

"Let's start there then since that is the most obvious," Anna said. "Read them out to me," Anna said as she turned the laptop toward her body. She tapped the computer keyboard and opened a web browser search engine and waited for Simon to read off the numbers.

"Okay, the first one is 4775 11120 7401, next is 5575 58376 173, then 5694 96241 052, and finally 5150 74012 78." Simon leaned over to see the results of the search with the numbers.

Anna sat back in her seat slightly dejected, "The results are for computer codes and internet file computing."

"Try the second page. I often find the best deals on items that show on the second or third pages when I am shopping," Simon suggested.

"Really?" Anna said, however, she gave it a try anyway. As she clicked the next button and the information from the second page scrolled across the screen, she was more interested.

"Look at the third number is showing for Riga," Simon pointed to the second entry on the page.

"Not just anything, the latitude, and longitude for Riga," Anna cleared the search page and entered the third figure separately, and confirmed that the numbers were identical to the capital city of Latvia. She entered the other account numbers one at a time and each time the first search result was the longitude and latitude for a city.

"Riga, London, Washington, and Moscow. All major cities. That's a bit more than a coincidence. Don't you think?" Simon said.

"Look at the last deposit. It was for Moscow. Maybe that is why Josh was there," Anna surmised.

"Look at the first deposit amount," Simon instructed, "It matches the date that Josh was in Moscow."

"What was the previous deposit?" Anna asked.

"It matches the longitude and latitude for Riga," Simon read the sheet a few seconds longer then looked at Anna. "And the first deposit would match the date that you were there, and that Logan met with Dr. Petrov."

"And the date I was attacked," Anna added.

"Then the second and third numbers must mean something as well," Simon said.

"$1,700 would match the time the wedding reception started if you convert it to military time." Anna noticed.

"And would $1,630 match up with the time that Logan met with Dr. Petrov?" Simon asked, already knowing what the answer would be.

Anna thought back to the day in Riga before she was attacked in the cemetery and nodded. It was around 4:30 in the afternoon that the two men met at the restaurant. "Then what would the last deposit amount represent? They are all four digits each time."

"A code perhaps. To make sure the person meeting was the right contact. We always used verbal codes," Simon said.

"William could never find a trace of any meeting or conversation that could involve Quantum or any of its agents. That was probably because they made sure there was no trail. The agents meeting up could easily log in to see the deposits made and attain the place and time to meet. The third deposit would ensure that the agent had the right code, even if they were being followed on their flight," Anna was sure they found what Josh was talking about.

"It's simple and not easy to trace either," Simon said.

Anna noticed two security guards as they ran out of the bank next door.

"What do you think that's about?" Anna asked.

Simon disconnected his jump drive from the computer and closed the lid to his laptop, "I think their system found my little tap." Simon slipped the laptop behind the cushion on the bench seat he was sitting on and as soon as the guards entered the café, he grabbed hold of Anna and pulled her in for a kiss.

Anna pushed him back and through clenched teeth said, "What do you think you're doing?"

Simon motioned with his eyes toward two guards that were making their way around the tables in the café and Anna then pulled Simon toward her and reengaged their kiss. She listened for their footsteps as they made their way around the restaurant. After a few minutes, the bell above the door rang as the two men left the café in search of their electronic intruder.

Anna and Simon pulled away from each other in unison once they were sure the two guards had left and quickly gathered their things and made their way to the car. Choosing not to mention the last couple of minutes or the kiss.

Anna pulled out one of the papers that the bank receptionist had given them and punched in the last address to her phone's GPS they had registered for Eloria.

As Simon drove to the last known address on file, Anna flipped through the two sheets of information and found three addresses, one of which was the same one on the back of the photograph she found in Denis's locker. She made a mental note to tell Simon about the picture.

"Anything interesting?" Simon asked.

"During the last couple of years that Eloria used this account to make deposits, there were also transactions to another account at the same bank in just her name alone. It looks like everything was emptied and transferred to an account in the U.S."

"Odd," Simon said.

Anna looked up as Simon drove down the narrow, cobblestone street and shouted, "There, number 41."

Simon pulled over to the side and once they parked, they hopped out and walked over to the address on the sheet.

It was a small stone house set back on the street about twenty feet. It was surrounded by a lush green lawn and edged with wildflowers. They unlatched the gate and walked up the stone path that led directly to the front door. They knocked on the door a couple of times before a young woman answered.

As she opened the door Anna could hear the television in the background as it entertained the laughing children with a musical cartoon.

Anna introduced herself as a cousin of a previous owner and then showed her a picture of Eloria that they received from the bank.

The young woman smiled at the photo and said that yes, she remembered buying the house from this woman. She was very happy to sell it to them because she wanted a young happy family living in the home.

When Anna asked if she knew where she could find Eloria the woman said, unfortunately, she could not. The woman moved to the U.S. and she didn't leave a forwarding address.

Anna thanked her and they returned to the car parked out front. Just before they reached the gate, the woman shouted after Anna and said she could try her brother. He used to visit, and she thinks he still lives in the old family home.

Simon and Anna got back into the car and Simon said, "Now there's a brother. We need to track down the family address."

Anna paused for a short second and then turned to face Simon, "I think I may know how we can find it."

Anna pulled out the photograph she had tucked inside her jacket pocket and handed it to Simon. "Turn it over," Anna instructed.

"This address is in Latvia?" Simon said.

"Yeah, I have the full address on this sheet," Anna pulled out a paper that Svetlana had printed for her the day before.

Simon looked at the address then flipped the photo over, "Where did you get this picture? It looks old."

Anna looked Simon in the eye and admitted, "I got it from Denis's locker at the safehouse."

CHAPTER 18–

"I forgot about the picture when I was telling you everything back at the hotel. I swear." Anna pleaded with Simon hoping he trusted her.

"I believe you," Simon said without hesitation. "What do you think it means?"

"I'd like to think it means that Denis was on the right track to finding out what was going on," Anna said.

"You think he was killed because he was getting close to the truth?" Simon asked.

Anna paused but then answered, "Yeah, I do."

"Okay, let's go see if we can find Eloria's brother," Simon said as he keyed in the address to his hand-held GPS device. The screen blinked as it configured the driving route and once it was completed, Simon began to follow the route on the screen.

They reached the address that was located about five miles outside of town just down a rural road. The property looked to be about six acres and the rolling field was mostly left wild being left unfarmed for many years. The wood fence that surrounded the property wore its age with cracks and bends from all the winters it fought to stay straight.

The stone house looked to be over a hundred years old and at first glance, it was obvious it would have been around for many many wars. Time was remarkably kind to the façade of the building considering it looked unmaintained for the last couple of decades. Except for unruly plants and trees, the building's structure was solid and showed no signs of cracking.

As Anna and Simon made their way around the building, they peered into the dirt-covered windows but could see no indication that anyone was living here or had, in fact, lived here in a long while.

"Sveiki! Vai varu jums palīdzēt?" The voice came from behind them.

Anna turned to face an elderly man as he made his way up the stone path to where she was standing.

"Do you speak English?" Anna said.

The man smiled and nodded, "German, Russian, English. Yes, with everyone who has been through these regions I've learned to speak many languages." The elderly man wore many years of sadness in the lines of his face, but he also had a glimmer of hope in his eyes that obviously was the driving force in keeping him alive.

"I'm looking for the family that may have lived here a while back," Anna held out a picture of Eloria that she had received from the bank earlier.

The man took the paper in his wrinkled, aged hand and a warm smile crossed his face. "You know Eloria?" His piercing blue eyes revealed he had a deep fondness for her.

"Yes, a long-lost cousin I was trying to track down. I am doing family research," Anna explained.

The sadness returned to the man's face as he handed the paper back to Anna, "I'm sorry you came all this way. She no longer lives here."

"Do you know where I could find her?" Anna asked, then added. "Or anyone else that may have lived here?"

The man shook his head. "Eloria moved away a long time ago. Her brother went before her. I think overseas, but I'm not sure."

Anna let out a dejected sigh. She needed to find Eloria and find out what her connection was to this and what it had to do with Denis.

"I'm sure you are here to try and make sense of everything that happened. It is so very sad. Senseless," The old man said.

Anna lifted her head in response to what the man said, Simon had returned by now from the other side of the property and was listening to their conversation. "What happened?"

"The family. Do you not know what happened to your own family?" The old man asked.

"No, sorry," Anna had to think quickly on her feet, "My father didn't want to speak of what happened, that's why I came all this way. He's dead now and I'd like to know more about our family history."

The old man seemed to soften at her words, "I understand why he would have found it difficult. Most of us still do. There were many times that this region was invaded by troops and the local farmers and villagers found themselves under the rule of either Germans or Russians. There were many atrocities during those times. Horrible crimes that I cannot speak of easily. We generally tried to stay out of any conflicts. We didn't have the means or the weapons to fight back, so our best defense was often to provide shelter and food to whoever was invading at that time. We fought when we could, but mostly we just survived. Latvia has often been caught in the middle of very violent conflicts and somehow we have survived but not without some loss of life.

"During one of the periods, the Evanishyn's became frustrated with the pressure of the Russian soldiers and Andris approached the American's who were here undercover and offered to help them. Andris and Inga just wanted to provide a good life for their kids. They wanted to keep them safe from harm. Andris was a good man and he was smart. He managed to infiltrate the Russians and gain valuable information that the Americans were able to use in their defense against them."

"What happened?" Anna asked.

"The Americans that Andris was dealing with promised they would take his family out of Latvia and bring them to America. However, when the Americans left they didn't contact Andris any further and once the Russians found out he had been the source of the American's information they killed him. Inga was left with the kids, broke and destitute.

After a particularly harsh winter, Inga became quite ill and died the next spring. The children were little and had to be separated to survive." A tear ran down the old man's face as he remembered the story.

Anna pulled the photograph from her pocket and handed it to the old man, "Were these the kids?"

The old man's tears were replaced with a smile and Anna caught a glimpse of how the man was able to survive with such sadness in his heart. He was able to capture moments of joy and hope amid great despair. "Yes, these were the kids."

"Were you very close to the kids?" Anna asked.

"Yes. However, I could never tell the boys apart," The old man handed the photo back to Anna. "One of the boys was adopted by a British couple and the other two went to live with an aunt in Riga, on Strasbourg."

Anna recognized the name of the street as the one that she and Simon were at earlier.

The man looked exhausted and turned to leave. Anna knew she had received all the information she could from the old man and let him return to what he was doing before she arrived.

She and Simon began to walk back to the car when Anna's phone buzzed from within her pocket. She reached in and pulled out her phone. She held it up to Simon and showed him it was Alastair that was calling.

Anna pressed the green button and held the phone up to her ear and answered the call, "Hi Alastair."

"Anna, where are you?" Alastair asked.

"In the middle of rural Latvia with Simon. We're following up on a lead," Anna explained.

"How is that turning out?" Alastair asked.

"Good actually, I'm learning to trust him again," Anna said as she smiled at Simon, who smiled back.

"Anna, I did some digging as you asked. I think I know why you wouldn't give me too many specifics. You wanted me to see it on my own. I can see why it was missed in the confusion. There were so many bodies found, and the craziness must have been overwhelming for the investigators," Alastair explained.

"What are you talking about Alastair?" Anna said.

"Most of the bodies were scorched, burnt beyond recognition. Dental records were the only way to identify most of the bodies. There were some bodies on the top floor that were not so badly damaged, those individuals were identified by their photos and security badges. Once they were able to match up the bodies with passes to the security log from that morning, those people were just struck from the list and the resources were spent trying to identify the more difficult cases," Alastair said.

"Did you find anything that the investigators missed?" Anna asked.

"Of course, I did. Why else would you have asked me?" Alastair said with a laugh. "If I wasn't looking for something out of place, I wouldn't have found it. I discounted the bodies that were identified with dental records and focused on the other bodies. The investigators took photos of each body they were able to identify visually. As you are aware, it's standard procedure to photograph the entire body, not just the face. I sent you the photo I found of Denis, it should be coming into your phone now."

Anna put the phone on speaker and pressed the screen and watched as the image appeared in front of her eyes. It was Denis. Laying in the rubble, eyes blackened and swollen from the weight of the crushing rock and his face and torso cut and bruised from the force of the explosion. "It's him. I have seen him enough to recognize him."

"Look closer, think of what brought you to Sergey. Don't focus on the fact you think it's Denis," Alastair said.

Anna placed her two fingers on the screen and dragged them apart zooming in on Denis's arm in the photo.

"There's no tattoo!" Simon exclaimed.

"Exactly! So that got me thinking. I had Sergey run a deeper level of the tissue sample you left him and compared it to the sample taken after the explosion, and it confirmed what I thought. The DNA came back as an initial match for Denis, however, when you take it a level deeper it shows it is not Denis but a close relation to him," Alastair explained.

"A twin," Anna said.

"Yes. Whoever that was in the explosion, it wasn't Denis, it was his brother."

CHAPTER 19-

"A twin!" Simon exclaimed, "Did you know he had a twin?"

"No, I didn't know much about him. He never seemed to want to talk about his family, so I just left it," Anna said.

"So that means this Eloria is his sister," Simon added. They were back in the car and making their way back to the city at a quicker pace than when they drove out.

"Yeah, I guess so. I would also guess that it was Denis that was adopted by the British family. He mentioned once he was in boarding school, but I don't think he was too fond of his time there. He had commented once about being an outsider the whole time he was at school."

"Did he ever talk about his family?" Simon asked,

"No, not really. He would let some things slip occasionally, like the boarding school comment, but other than that nothing," Anna said. "There was once he had made a comment about having it hard growing up and that we would never understand. I just blew it off as his way of joking around. You know how sometimes Denis would have a dry sense of humor. I just thought it was like that. I never knew."

"Well whatever the reason, it doesn't explain why his brother was in the explosion and why his sister is involved with a banking account that Ashbury and his team and Quantum Security have been using," Simon blurted out.

"You're right Simon. It just doesn't make any sense," Anna said.

"Well, this means two things," Simon said.

"What's that?" Anna asked.

"That Denis is still alive and that he is probably not on our side. He could be mixed up in this whole thing," Simon knew that Anna was going to have a tough time dealing with the knowledge that her partner that she mourned for all those months was not only alive but had tried to hurt her.

"We need to see Ashbury. Right now! I think he is the only one who can clear this up," Anna said.

Simon screeched the car to a stop causing the rear tires to weave to a stop along the gravel road.

Anna threw her hands against the dashboard to keep from hitting her head, "What was that for?"

Simon pointed to an old worn-out sign that was tilted on an angle from a combination of both age and neglect. It stood in front of a lake bordered with thick clumps of Silver Birch on the opposite side. The side that Simon and Anna were on had a long grassy lawn that led up to a beach that held an equal mix of rock and sand. The wind blew small white caps over the surface of the water and the water colliding with the low rocks made a soothing rhythmic sound that conjured up memories of summer vacations at the cottage.

Simon pointed to the dilapidated sign that caught his attention and then opened the driver's side door and stepped out onto the gravel road. He walked around the front of the car and made his way over toward the sign as Anna opened her door and began to follow him. Simon was walking straight toward a sign with the words 'Burtnieks' etched in faded wood that Anna would have disregarded. The lake was large and if Anna had to guess it was over five miles long. Simon had now stopped next to the sign and she stood beside him as he read it.

"Want to tell me why you stopped here?" Anna asked.

"Let me see that picture you have," Simon asked with his hand stretched out toward Anna.

Anna reached into her pocket and pulled out the photo of the young kids that Anna now believed were Denis and his family. She handed it to Simon and waited while he looked at it. Simon held the photo in his left hand and then held it up in front of their faces and flicked the corner with two fingers on his right hand.

"See," he exclaimed. "This is where the photo was taken."

Anna leaned in next to Simon's shoulder and looked at the photo and then to the horizon where Simon was pointing. He was right. The landscape had changed slightly over time, however, there was no mistaking this location as the one where the photo was taken.

"I agree. But I don't see how this helps us," Anna said.

Simon leaned down and began to read the tourist plaque that was affixed to a post that was positioned in the ground next to the sign for the lake.

"What does it say?" Anna asked Simon.

"It's a story about a legend associated with this lake. It says there is a monster that lives on the bottom of the lake. During the numerous invasions of Russians and Germans, the monster was known to rise up and capture the oppressors and bring them to the bottom of the lake for them to spend eternity in suffering," Simon looked at Anna and raised his eyebrows and then continued. "The legend has it that any who bring evil or darkness to the people of the land will suffer the wrath of the 'blackwater'."

"Blackwater?" Anna asked

"That's what it says," Simon confirmed. "Also, the English translation for the name of the lake is 'eater'."

Anna looked out onto the lake as the water lapped the small waves upon the rocky shore, "Seems like a bit much of a coincidence that Josh had a secret file with the name Blackwater on it, and that it turns out to be where this photo was taken and found in Denis's locker."

"Now would be a good time to get William on the phone and fill him in on what you know. I understand that you've had a few curve balls sent your way and you're still figuring out who to trust, but you need to trust William," Simon said and then turned to Anna. "After all, if you can trust me, then you can trust William."

Anna knew Simon was right. While Simon drove them toward the airport in Riga, Anna called William and brought him up to date on the events of the past few days. Including what she knew about Denis. This time she didn't leave anything out. It took her about half an hour to explain everything and for the three of them to work out a plan on how to approach Ashbury. By the time Anna was finished speaking with William, she was exhausted. There was even a time that she once believed that she and Denis could even have been a couple. She never crossed that line, thinking it was her sense of professionalism that held her back. In hindsight, she must have had an idea that she couldn't believe in who she thought Denis really was. They reached the airport and made their way to the private jet runway. William had arranged for a jet to be fueled and waiting for them when they arrived. Simon and Anna were seated and the jet was in the air moments later. Anna had connected her computer to the plane's power system and began to review the files that Simon had received from his source and the information that Svetlana was able to retrieve from the encrypted files. Suddenly Anna stopped and looked up at Simon.

"What?" Simon asked.

"What if the information I got from Svetlana was a setup?" Anna thought out loud.

"What is your gut feeling?" Simon asked.

"That she was being genuine. I don't think she had any idea that Denis is alive. And so far, the information she gave us turned out to be valuable," Anna said. "Sorry. I guess I'm just second-guessing myself now."

"Don't do that Anna. You're a great agent," Simon said. "Plus, you're just going to get us killed thinking like that." Simon winked at Anna and then returned to reading the files on his screen.

Anna grinned and returned to her research. An hour into the flight and Anna closed her laptop screen, pressing down until she heard a clicking lock sound.

"What did you find on Ashbury?" Anna asked, knowing that Simon was tracking Ashbury so they could plan to catch him off guard.

"He's in Washington now. A state dinner has been arranged for the Russians and it's taking place in one day, right after a private board meeting that's been scheduled," Simon said. "I think we should get him at his house."

"No. A guy like Ashbury will be guarded to the hilt," Anna tapped her finger on the laptop in front of her. "Does he go to a gym at all?"

Simon tapped away at his computer and nodded, "You're good. He is a member of a racquet club not far from his home. I can get us in there a lot easier, and the chances of there being a ton of security are slim."

Anna stared out the window at the sky which was turning a light shade of purple with the rising sun in the distance.

"What's bothering you?" Simon asked.

"What do you mean?" Anna said.

"I know that look," Simon trailed off hoping Anna would reveal what she was thinking.

"It's Eloria. I can't help but think she looks extremely familiar." Anna admitted.

"Well, she is his sister. Maybe it is just a family resemblance," Simon offered.

"Maybe," Anna decided to put Denis and his two mysterious siblings out of his mind. At least for now. She decided to get a bit of rest for the remainder of the flight and quickly nodded off to sleep.

The last thing she remembered before she closed her eyes was seeing Simon watch her as she slowly floated away.

CHAPTER 20-

Anna felt the weight of Simon's hand on her arm as he gently shook her awake.

"We're about to land. You may want to wake up," Simon was kneeling beside Anna's seat and had both hands on her arm. She found she liked the feeling of him being near. He made her feel safe again.

Anna sat up straight and wiped the sleep from her eyes. "What time is it?" she asked.

"Almost ten o'clock in the morning," Simon said.

"Do you ever sleep?" Anna joked.

"I caught a little bit of sleep. But I wanted to make sure we were ready when we landed," Simon explained.

"What time does Ashbury go to his club?" Anna asked.

"We are in luck. He has a personal training session planned for noon today. We can get him just as he is getting ready," Simon explained.

"Good, maybe we can finally figure out who is behind this and put a stop to it for good. And then William can come out of hiding," Anna said.

Anna began to feel the sensation of the plane losing altitude as they began their descent into Washington. She packed up her laptop and tucked her gear into her bag. She picked up the muffin that was sitting on her tray from the beginning of the flight and began to pick pieces off the top and popped them into her mouth. She worked to chew the stale pieces so she would be able to swallow them without choking. Anna looked over at Simon and caught him watching her.

"What?" she said.

"Remind me to buy you a proper meal when we are done?" Simon joked.

"Deal," Anna finished the muffin and prepared for the landing.

Once they began to taxi to the waiting SUV that William arranged, Anna and Simon began to grab their bags and stand in the plane. The plane came to a complete stop and the pilot released the latch on the door and pushed it up as the stairs lowered simultaneously to the ground.

Anna thanked the pilot for a smooth flight and she and Simon made their way to the waiting SUV. They began to drive toward the exit when the phone in Anna's pocket rang. She pulled it out and saw that William was calling.

Anna answered the call and put it on speaker, "William, we just arrived."

"I know, who do you think arranged the flight?" William said.

Anna raised her eyebrows at Simon and they both smiled.

"I assume you are in the car by now," William said.

"Yes, we're on our way to Ashbury's racquet club now. Any idea of who he is meeting at this board meeting later?" Anna asked.

"Not specifics. The agenda is tight. They're a security firm by the way, so it is not as easy to work around their system. Also, Ashbury is not even supposed to technically be involved with Quantum, so I'm not even sure if he will be showing up," William added.

"Well, he still has information that'll be valuable," Anna added.

"Let's hope so," William added. "Even though I couldn't get the agenda, there is a curious list of Russians and Syrian's flying into Washington today. Not sure if it's for the meeting or the state dinner."

"Or both," Simon added.

"Yes, or both," William said. "Abramovich is on the list of those flying in, along with Nizar al-Noury."

"The Syrian defense minister?" Anna asked.

"That's the one. He has been at complete odds with the Americans over his handling of the refugees in his country and the outlying regions. He has been accused of using them to run contraband out of the country, among other atrocities," William explained. "Not exactly sure why he's even allowed into the country, let alone how he managed it under the radar of the press."

"Maybe our friend Ashbury can shed some light on the list once we reach him," Anna said.

Then in an instant, the midnight blue Charger that was traveling in front of them screeched to a halt. Simon hit the brakes and had to swerve to miss rear-ending the car. Simon came to a stop beside the car and looked inside the window of the vehicle that came to an abrupt stop in front of them. He and Anna caught sight of the black metal at the same moment the driver turned to face them.

"Simon, go!" Anna screamed.

Simon hit the accelerator as the driver of the Charger raised what looked like a small grenade launcher out through his driver's side window toward the black SUV.

The shot from the weapon tore off a rear light and sent a shock through the vehicle causing it to weave on the balance of the four tires.

Simon steadied the car with his strength while Anna pulled out her gun and cocked the chamber. The SUV swerved left and right moving around the other cars moving in the same direction, but completely unaware of the danger in pursuit of the black SUV.

"Head down 66!" Anna shouted while she grabbed the handle above the door and swiveled in her seat and watched the Charger along with a speeding Expedition make their way through the traffic behind them at great speed.

"There are two of them now," Anna shouted.

Anna watched as the Expedition plowed into the back of a small compact car, sending it spinning into the traffic, and then it accelerated past the pile of cars inching closer to Anna and Simon's SUV.

The Charger was taking advantage of its smaller size and sped along the shoulder passing everyone in its way until it was only a car length behind Anna and Simon.

Simon drove with incredible skill as he moved around small and large vehicles narrowly missing bumpers and hoods bringing them closer to the off-ramp. They were within 400 meters of the exit when Anna saw a body extend out of the passenger side of the Charger which was now directly behind them.

Anna wrapped the seat belt around her left arm and hung out the window of the SUV and aimed at the Charger that was gaining speed. Simon was traveling at ninety-five miles an hour and with Anna hanging out the window it would take an expert shot to hit the Charger and not any of the other vehicles on the road.

Anna's first shot ricocheted off the hood doing very little to slow them down. Her next shot hit the windshield just as the passenger from the Charger released a barrage of fire from the weapon he hung out of his window.

"What the hell was that?" Simon asked as he watched the road in front of him as well as frequently glancing at the mirror watching the cars in pursuit.

"I have no bloody idea. I've never seen a gun like that before," Anna shouted.

"Go old school," Simon shouted.

"I don't want to hurt anyone around him!" Anna yelled.

"Too late," Simon revved the engine lurching the SUV further into the next lane as soon as he saw an opening.

Anna leaned out the window and steadied the gun as she aimed at the front passenger tire. The first shot landed perfectly in the center of the tread blowing the tire off the rim. The Charger veered left then right compensating for the loss of traction on the road. Anna's second shot landed in the middle of the driver's side of the windshield, leaving a clean hole before the driver had a chance to steady the car any further. Anna's third shot took out the rear passenger tire and sent the Charger into a wild tailspin.

The Charger hit three other cars traveling in the same direction as it spun out of control.

Finally, the black metal screeched as the car slid along the cement barrier that edged the freeway until the car was moving backward at an alarming rate. Anna was sure she also hit the diver because he was not attempting to slow the car down. She watched as the car slammed into a pile of safety barrels forcing the front of the car into the air and above the ground about thirty feet. The force of the car slamming into the pile of barrels at that speed sent the car into two full spins in the air before it landed on the roof and slid the final distance spinning around in circles until it crashed into a semi-trailer parked on the side of the highway and burst into flames.

Simon continued off the exit and raced his way into the city. The Expedition had been able to close the distance between them while Anna was shooting at the Charger. Anna reloaded her gun and Simon pulled his from his jacket and shoved it in her lap, "Here, you may need this."

As Anna watched, the Expedition slammed into cars in its path without the same concern she had for avoiding innocent victims being hurt.

Anna pushed the button above her head and opened the sunroof of the SUV.

She balanced herself with one foot on her seat and the other on the center console. She leaned her body forward resting on the roof of the car and fired her weapon at the windshield. Each shot ricocheted off the window.

"It's bulletproofed!" Anna shouted down to Simon.

Anna repositioned her gun and aimed at the front grill of the Expedition. Just as she was about to pull the trigger, the driver of the Expedition accelerated and rammed into the back of the SUV. The bullet from Anna's gun hit the roof of the Expedition leaving little more than a dent and as the force of the Expedition rammed the SUV it sent her body flying into the opposite end of the open sunroof slamming her back against the edge of the roof.

Anna screamed as the pain shot up her back.

She dropped one of the guns next to her foot on the seat and with her left hand, she grabbed the roof rack and pulled her body forward, and aimed the gun with her right hand.

"Gun it now!" Anna screamed at Simon.

Simon responded by lowering the accelerator to the ground and Anna could feel the strength of the motor as it reverberated through the seat and console that she was standing on.

When Simon had pulled a good distance from the Expedition, she fired three perfect shots in repetition that entered through the front grill and hit the engine block and the front of the Expedition erupted into flames.

Anna watched as the Expedition veered off to the left in a fiery mass as it collided with the cement barrier on the edge of the highway.

Anna slipped back down into the SUV and sat back in the passenger seat as Simon turned off the exit ramp.

They could hear the sirens behind them as the emergency crews began to arrive at the multiple accidents.

Anna reached up and pressed the button to close the sunroof muffling the sound of the sirens behind them and began to think what their next move should be.

CHAPTER 21-

Twenty minutes after Simon pulled off the freeway, he and Anna were sitting in the SUV a block away from the fitness club where Ashbury had scheduled a personal training session for that day.

"What time was Ashbury's session booked for today?" Simon asked.

"Twelve thirty. Sharp," Anna answered.

"Well, I better get in there now. I wouldn't want to keep Mr. Ashbury waiting," Simon slipped his revolver into his holster and opened the door to the SUV. "Give me about ten minutes after I go in to get him situated and then we will meet as planned."

"Got it," Anna answered as Simon stepped out of the vehicle.

Simon waited next to the parking area designated for staff and as the personal trainer's blue Mazda pulled into the lot, he knelt to the ground and began to tie his lace. He waited patiently as the Mazda pulled into the spot next to where

Simon was waiting and then just as the car door was opening Simon stood and began to walk over to the driver.

"Hi there, I was wondering if you could help me?" Simon flashed a smile and held out his hand to greet the young driver.

"Sure, what can I do for you?" the young man answered, returning the greeting.

"I have a session with one of the members, but I seem to have forgotten the passcode to get in. Are you heading in now?" Simon asked.

"Yeah, man. But I am not allowed to let anyone in. You know security and all," the young driver began to walk away.

"Hey, no problem man. Could you get a message to Mr. Faust?" Simon asked.

The young man stopped mid-step and turned to face Simon, "John Faust?"

"Yeah, do you know him?" Simon asked.

"Every trainer in town knows who he is. Ever since he picked up his third ball team, he's been looking for staff to work with them."

"Yeah," Simon said, "I have a session with him today and I was going to help him pick the trainers he was going to ask to come aboard the team roster."

Simon was sure he could see the wheels turning in the young trainer's head, "I can probably get you in as my assistant."

"Awesome, you would be doing me a huge favor," Simon began to walk beside the young man and slapped him on the back, "I'll put a good word in for you. What's your name?"

"Max Allen," the young man answered. "You have no idea how much I would appreciate it. Some of the clients I have are a huge pain. Like the guy that I'm supposed to be training today."

As the two walked toward the front door Simon asked him, "Oh really, who are you training today?"

"Some guy named Ashbury. He's loaded and out of shape so he hires guys like me to stroke his ego."

Simon held the door open and said, "I hear you."

Once the two were cleared from the front desk staff, Simon followed Max to the trainer's office area. Simon made sure there was no one else in the room and then closed the door behind him.

"Hey, listen, I kind of lied to you out there," Simon confessed.

"Lied how?" Max said as he dropped his bag on the bench. "Do you even know Faust?"

"Oh yeah, I know him. But the interviews are later today for the team." Simon said.

"Great, another opportunity I am going to miss because I have to work crazy training sessions with wannabe athletes." Max sighed, "Oh well, thanks anyway."

"Hey, I didn't say you weren't in," Simon reached into his back pocket and pulled out a card, and handed it to Max. "Be at this address today in an hour and I guarantee you'll not only get an interview, but you'll get hired."

Max grabbed the card with Faust's personal office contact information imprinted on the front in raised gold letters. "You're serious?"

"Absolutely," Simon responded.

Max looked at the card and then at the schedule board that had his name marked beside Ashbury's.

Simon quickly said, "Look, I'll take care of that guy. This is a once-in-a-lifetime opportunity. Don't blow it."

Max nodded and then smiled as he grabbed his bag, "I'll do it. Thanks, I don't know how I will ever repay you."

"Get the team in shape this year so they can finally win a season," Simon said.

Max quickly left the room before he could change his mind and left Simon standing in the trainer's office alone. He pulled out his phone and pulled up the contact information for Faust who picked up on the second ring.

"Simon, how are you, buddy?" Faust greeted into the phone.

"I am great John. How is that shoulder of yours doing?" Simon asked his old college roommate.

"Ah, you know. Not good. But that is why I own the team and don't play on it," John chuckled.

"I need a favor John," Simon asked.

"Anything," Faust replied.

"I am sending a young guy by the name of Max Allen over to your office. He'll be there in an hour or so. He's coming to interview for one of the trainer positions with the team."

"Simon, you know I already have selected the guys for those positions," Faust explained.

"Give this guy a shot John. He is a good kid and I owe him one," Simon looked at his watch and noticed he had less than five minutes to get into position for Ashbury.

Faust let out a sigh, "Okay Simon if you say this kid is worth a shot, I'll take him on."

Simon then said, "Great, but don't let him know how you really know me. Just tell him,"

"Yeah, I know, just like always, you're my trainer!" Faust laughed and made Simon promise to drop by for a beer before he left town.

Simon had just enough time to make it to the backroom before Anna got there. He grabbed a rubber exercise band from the equipment basket on his way into the private gym that Ashbury had booked for his session. As Simon entered the room, he could see the back of Ashbury's head as he attempted a leg stretch on the floor mat at the opposite end of the room.

"Mr. Ashbury," Simon announced as he entered the room.

Ashbury turned to face Simon and narrowed his eyes and creased his brow as he stood, "Where's Max?"

"Max couldn't make it today. I am filling in for him," Simon said. He stood with his legs spread shoulder-width apart and was positioned between Ashbury and the door. Simon's hands were folded behind his back with the exercise band held taught.

"I am going to call my office quickly to make sure this has been approved," Ashbury began to walk toward the door when Simon stepped sideways blocking his path.

"Move aside," Ashbury ordered.

"But we just began," Anna said from behind where Ashbury was standing, causing him to spin on his feet to face her.

Anna had entered the room from the service entrance while Simon had distracted Ashbury. Simon was in the process of locking the door of the room as Anna was doing the same with the door she entered from.

"What is the meaning of this!" Ashbury shouted. He dashed toward his gym bag and reached in and pulled out his cell phone.

He began to punch the numbers of his security detail waiting in the parking lot when Simon held up a small black square box, "Don't bother. I brought a jammer with me."

Ashbury dropped his phone in his bag and held his hands out, "What is it you want? You know you won't be able to get me out of here. My detail is instructed to kill on sight. No negotiations. We'll all be dead in minutes."

"Oh, we don't plan on taking you anywhere," Anna walked a little closer to where Ashbury was standing. "We just need some answers from you."

"Answers for what?" Ashbury said.

"This," Anna threw down the files of information she and Simon had amassed over the past couple of days. "Bank records, emails, transfers – they all lead back to you. And Quantum."

Ashbury leaned over and brushed his hands over the papers moving them aside to quickly glance at their contents. He then shrugged. "So, all these files show is that you have some banking information and some random emails. Disgruntled employees, I am sure. Nothing points to me."

"We found Logan," Anna blurted out.

Ashbury's face drained, "Who?"

"Logan James, your man on the inside. I followed him to Riga," Anna stared straight-faced into Ashbury's eyes.

"I don't know who you are talking about. You must have made some mistake." A bead of sweat began to trickle down Ashbury's forehead and his pupils rapidly dilated. He was doing anything he could to not reveal that he knew who Logan James was.

"I got the vial before he was killed," Anna lied.

Ashbury's eyebrows raised as he stood motionless, refusing to break eye contact with Anna, "I told you I don't know what you're talking about."

"So, you weren't interested in the vial that Dr. Petrov was selling Logan?" Anna said.

"Who are you?" Ashbury finally said.

"Someone who has something you want," Anna crossed her arms. "What's it worth to you?"

Ashbury slowly allowed a smirk to creep across his face, "So this is what this is all about?" Ashbury walked over and sat on the bench next to his bag. "Extortion?"

Anna decided to let Ashbury speak, hopefully revealing information she would find useful.

When Ashbury realized Anna was not ready to say anything further, he shook his head and said, "What is it you want. Name your price."

"Information," Anna said.

"Information! You really don't know what that vial is worth then," Ashbury held his hands over his face and yelled into his hands. "I knew I should never have trusted Logan. He was an idiot!"

"Why don't you start with telling me what Quantum Security has to do with all these emails and bank accounts?" Anna nodded toward the pile of paper she threw down on the bench.

Ashbury picked up the papers and laughed as he flipped through them, "Looks like you found Josh as well."

Anna's chest tightened at the sound of Josh's name. She was still saddened by his death. But now wasn't the time to show that. She just nodded.

"Seems like you have everything here. What can I tell you?" Ashbury said.

"String it together for me why don't you," Anna said.

"May as well. As soon as we are done, you're as good as dead. My guys will hunt you down and you'll be finished." Ashbury threatened.

Just then Simon wrapped the rubber exercise band around Ashbury's neck and pulled on the ends cutting off the flow of air to his lungs.

As Ashbury kicked and squirmed his face began to turn from a shade of red to purple as his body was slowly being deprived of oxygen. Just before he was about to pass out, Simon loosened his grip allowing just enough air into Ashbury's lungs to revive him.

"Are you crazy!" Ashbury screamed.

"Tell me your sordid little story with Quantum and my friend here will leave you alone," Anna instructed.

"Okay, okay," Simon released the rubber exercise band but continued to stand behind Ashbury as a warning. "It goes back a few generations as you probably already know. My family has been in the security business for quite some time. Over that period Quantum has created a lot of contacts in various countries. We offer security services to government officials, company executives. Basically, anyone who can pay our price."

"How does Seaforth fit into your story?" Anna asked.

"The Seaforth? Now you are going back a bit. That was a Russian trolling ship that was hiding out in Swedish waters. It was our job to keep it there unnoticed until the Russians were ready to use it. We got it there disguised as a British ship and just waited for orders from the Russians," Ashbury explained.

"What was on the ship?" Anna asked.

"Plans for the war, the city layout, and ammunition stores. Things like that," Ashbury said.

"You don't seem to have a problem with that," Anna said.

"It was a job, that's all," Ashbury said. "I couldn't change how the war was going to turn out."

"What happened then," Anna asked.

"Some workers aboard the ship snuck off into town. They got drunk and some locals heard them speaking Russian when they were in the back of a bar. The authorities were notified and when they followed the two back to the boat – that was it. We were done."

Anna grabbed the bank statements and stock reports that Simon had obtained from his contact. "How does all that relate to these?"

"Our business grew over the years and began to take on a different view. We began to take an interest in the market and saw how easily we could manipulate it if we were in control of cargo from certain countries. The bank accounts were used as a means of contact for our various agents. Like Logan. They told them where to meet, and at what time. Once the agent arrived in the city, they went to the designated hotel room and the instructions for their job were left in the room."

"The third number was the room?" Anna said.

"It was pretty simple. I guess now we are going to have to adjust our process a little," Ashbury said as he looked at Anna and Simon and the papers she held in her hands.

"How did you affect the markets?" Anna asked.

"Depends on the region and the cargo we were moving. Sometimes it was a lost ship, a water system in a large city sabotaged, or even planting false information so rebels within warring countries would revolt against each other. We had a few companies that each owned a small percentage of the shares. However, because they were all controlled by Quantum, we held majority control of the companies from behind the scenes. We could do what we wanted with each one."

"Like in Latvia," Anna was putting it together now.

"Exactly," Ashbury said, "Getting the Russian's and German's to fight with each other was easy enough. And we just sat back and handed off weapons to both sides. We controlled the oil in the region, the utilities, everything."

Anna shook her head, "How can you live with yourself?"

"Quite well actually," Ashbury leaned back on his hands crossing his ankles. "Now that I am in government, I can help create political tensions between countries for trade, and then Quantum or one of our many subsidiaries swoops in and fixes the problem for a price."

"What did you have to do with the explosion at the Special Division Unit under the Command of William Lewis?" Anna asked.

"So that is what this is all about. Are you one of his old agents?" Ashbury asked. "Now this makes sense."

Ashbury began to stand, "We're done here."

Simon lunged from behind Ashbury and once again tightened the band around his neck. As Ashbury struggled Simon whispered into his ear, "What did you have to do with the explosion?"

Simon lifted Ashbury off the ground with his strength and then as he released his grip on the bands, Ashbury came crashing to the ground with a thud. Ashbury coughed and grabbed the base of his neck as he crawled away from where Simon was standing.

He turned on his back and raised a hand in the air toward Simon, "William's team was getting too close. They had tracked Logan to a meeting in Riga and were pretty sure that he was involved in a stock manipulating scheme involving Russia. William had come to the executive branch to get special approval to follow that lead. Since his division didn't officially exist, and he only reported to the Executive Branch of the government, the request began and ended there."

"How did you know about it?" Anna asked.

"Who do you think sat on the Executive Branch at that time?" Ashbury smiled. "Once I realized that William was getting too close, I had no choice."

Anna lunged at Ashbury and wrapped her hands around his neck and began to squeeze as hard as she could.

Ashbury fought with all his might and the weight of his body pulled her to the ground where they continued to struggle. Simon pulled Anna off Ashbury, "Don't do it, Anna. He is going to pay. He needs to answer for what he did."

Anna stepped back, her hands shaking with anger.

Anna had suddenly noticed fierce banging on the door, she wasn't sure how long it had been going on.

"That must be Ashbury's security!" Simon yelled.

"Anna. Simon. Open up!" William's voice boomed through the locked door.

Simon ran to the door and unlocked it, letting William inside.

"You!" Ashbury yelled.

"You're done Ashbury. I've been tracking you for years now and you're finally coming down once we reveal you for the traitor you are," William soon next to Simon, and judging by his heavy breathing, Anna had guessed that he had run full out from where he parked his car.

"You should've been killed in that explosion!" Ashbury yelled as spittle ran from the corner of his mouth. "Along with all your other bothersome agents. Too bad this one wasn't in the building," Ashbury nodded toward Anna who was still standing behind him.

"Too bad for you that I wasn't. Now your schemes of setting tariffs while controlling goods are over," Anna gloated.

Ashbury lunged toward his gym bag and pulled out his gun and before he could be stopped had aimed it directly at Anna.

"You're the one who is done. I'm getting out of here and when my security guards are done with you there won't be a trace," Ashbury threatened all three as he waved the gun between Simon and Anna.

William and Simon pulled out their guns when Ashbury turned his focus on Anna.

"You try anything and this one gets a bullet right in the head," Ashbury yelled.

"Put down your gun Ashbury," William yelled.

"No! I have too much invested in this. Do you even know what the guys are like that I deal with?" Ashbury shook his head. "This time I'm going to make sure you stay out of my way William!"

Ashbury pointed his gun toward William and squeezed the trigger. Anna lunged at Ashbury wrapping both her hands around his gun and raising his arm in the air. The two struggled as Ashbury tried to pull the gun out of Anna's grip.

William and Simon held their guns pointed at Ashbury and as Simon ran toward Anna and Ashbury, Ashbury broke free of Anna's grip and aimed the gun at Simon, and pulled the trigger.

The bullet ricocheted off Simon's shoulder sending him back over the bench. He turned the gun on Anna and pulled the trigger and the sound of the shot echoed in the room.

Anna watched as Ashbury bent forward losing his balance. William stood behind him with his gun pointed at Ashbury which was still hot from the shot. Ashbury collapsed to the ground and William ran and held Anna in his arms.

"Are you alright?" William asked Anna as she clung to his body.

They hadn't seen Ashbury raise his arm toward William from where he lay on the ground.

William gasped for air and Simon fired a final shot into Ashbury.

"No! No! No!" Anna yelled as she tried her best to hold William upright. She could no longer fight the weight and with Simon's help, she lowered him to the ground.

The tears flowed from her eyes as she wiped the side of William's face.

"Stay with us! We will call for help!" Anna instructed, but Simon was already connected with emergency personnel.

William grabbed Anna's hand and as he struggled for air he began to speak to Anna, "I am sorry I hid my plan from you for so long. Can you forgive me?"

"Yes, you know I will. You're like a second father to me," Anna sobbed.

"Your dad was a hero Anna. He saved my life. You know that right," William sputtered.

Anna nodded.

"You need to know the whole story. I didn't tell you everything," William was struggling now for air.

Anna wrapped her arms around the base of his neck, she couldn't let him go, she wasn't sure she could handle losing him again.

"Relax, William. I know what happened. Just conserve your energy," Anna said.

"No, you don't know what happened. Not everything anyway. Your dad and I found something else on that ship that day. There was a stowaway. A Latvian man who was working as a spy for the U.S. government. He was one of our guys and we had to conceal his identity to keep him safe. He was an engineer for the government and at the time the Russian's had just invaded Latvia. They were an oppressive regime and the locals had very little in the way of support to fight any of their tactics. That is when we approached him and encouraged him to work for us. He agreed and we promised to get him and his family out of Latvia when the time came."

William coughed and as Anna tried to hold him down, he began to speak again.

"Once the government was toppled the area was a ruin. The economy had crumbled and it was horrible for those left behind. Especially in the rural areas. It was time to get Andris and his family out, but our government wouldn't keep its promise. Turns out they made more than one promise to people in the region and when it was time to honor it, they just left them there," William took a deep breath and let out a cough.

"What happened next?" Anna asked.

"Your dad and I tried to get him and his family out, but we were stopped at every angle. By the time we got approval and went to Latvia, both he and his wife had died."

Anna wiped tears from her eyes and held on tight to William as he continued to speak.

"Andris lost all hope of a future and took his own life. When we arrived, their children were being watched by a family member, but they only had enough money to keep two of them. We reluctantly agreed to take one and find a new life for him. We never wanted to separate the kids and our whole life we regretted it. We tried to keep track of the family but somewhere along the line, we lost track of the two left in Latvia. The one we took was placed with a family in England. He finished school and had a good family."

"What was the family's name?" Anna asked.

"Andris and Inga Evanishyn. The boy we extracted was Vladyslav Evanishyn. But you eventually grew to know him as Denis," William said.

Anna closed her eyes. Denis's involvement was becoming clear.

"You need to find Denis, I tried to help him, but I think I'm the reason this whole thing started," William said.

"What thing?" Anna asked.

"Blackwater."

CHAPTER 22-

After the ambulances had taken away the lifeless bodies of both William and Ashbury, Anna and Simon were separated and interviewed by the Director of Special Investigations for Internal Bureaus.

Neither the investigators nor Anna and Simon knew exactly where to begin. The most obvious place was to start explaining why William, whom the agency thought was dead, was alive.

Anna gave as simple an explanation as she could, trying her best to shine the light toward Ashbury's involvement as opposed to William's deceit. She wasn't sure what Simon's approach was going to be, but after the last few days she had become to see a different view of Simon and she was pretty sure he was going to do the same thing.

"So, you are saying that Ashbury is involved in an international scheme to control the market?" the agent asked Anna, trying his best to summarize a completely confusing story.

"No, not exactly. His family has run Quantum Security for a couple of generations. The security company started out by protecting high-level individuals, you know execs for companies and politicians from various countries." Anna leaned her head forward and paused to ensure that the agent was following her story.

The agent nodded and then Anna continued.

"I'm not sure exactly when but Quantum began to transport goods for less than reputable countries. Those that would be considered enemies of the U.S."

"That is a pretty big accusation to make. Especially since it involves one of the countries most decorated politicians," the agent added.

"I know. Believe me, it was a shock to me as well," Anna explained.

"I am assuming you have proof," the agent said. He just sat and listened and had stopped taking notes quite a while ago.

"Yes, of course. We have a trail that leads directly to Ashbury. It is a pretty convoluted one, but that is why William had to go undercover to investigate," Anna explained.

"We'll get to Agent Lewis later. Now, back to Ashbury transporting goods for enemy countries. Give me an example," the agent said.

"It involved so many different things, but they started small with cargo like drugs and guns," Anna explained.

"You call that small?" the agent asked.

"Well, when you compare it to what they took on later, yes," Anna crossed her arms. She tried her best not to sound terse with the agent.

"Okay, continue," the agent said.

"Well, like I said it started small then Quantum realized there was a huge market for them because of the connections and routes they had established around the world. Over time Quantum, through their subsidiaries, bought up quite a few companies and around the world. Some even controlled utilities in certain countries. Once Ashbury was elected Senator he had more say in restrictions and tariffs imposed by the U.S. and he was able to control the flow of goods in and out of the country from an arms reach – so to say," Anna waited to see if the agent was still on the same page. He nodded for her to continue.

"Then, when Ashbury made it to the Executive Branch of the government, he had complete knowledge of all the agencies. Like ours, and since Agent Lewis reported directly to the Executive, no one else in the government even knew we existed. Ashbury became aware that we were getting close to cracking his operation and moved to have the agency taken out," Anna suddenly felt a pain in the center of her stomach when she thought back to the day of the explosion.

"And Mr. James, he worked for Ashbury?" the agent asked remembering back to the initial explanation that Anna gave.

Anna nodded, "Yes. He ran many of the deposits in Riga while he was on business travel."

"Yes. The codes you were explaining. How did you break that again?" The agent's tone indicated he was more interested than doubtful.

Anna thought back to when she and Simon were in the café and the bank's security guards came in to search for the computer hacker that was scanning the bank files.

"We just did. Consider it years of experience that let us see more than just the numbers," Anna explained.

The agent raised his eyebrows, "Pretty impressive. I'm sure it is going to go into the training book after this," the agent paused. "You also mentioned Mr. Collins' involvement in all of this. Can you explain what happened in Russia?"

"It's like I said. Josh's girlfriend was completing research on her graduate degree when she came across some files that connected a few enemy countries with Quantum. It was a stretch but as she dug further, she found the connection so she decided to mail the evidence to Josh and he received it a few days later. Just after he found out she was killed in the parking lot of the University. It was ruled a carjacking gone wrong, but Josh thought it was too much of a coincidence," Anna took a drink of water from the bottle the EMT handed her when they first arrived. "When Josh brought the papers to William, they had decided it was worth a follow-up. William used Josh's extraordinary forensic accounting skills to get him infiltrated into one of Quantum's subsidiaries on the guise that he was distraught over the loss of his girlfriend and needed a less stressful job."

"So, Josh Collins was a good guy in all of this?" the agent asked.

"Very much so," Anna asserted.

The investigator closed his notebook and handed Anna his card, "Come in and we will type all this up. I think it is going to take more than a short interview to sort his out."

Anna agreed, and almost two hours after the investigators initially arrived, they let Anna and Simon leave with a promise to follow up on their statements. Anna could see that the agent she was speaking with had wished he hadn't come into work today. There was no way she would have wanted to be the one to try and sort this paperwork out, after all, she was on the inside and found it confusing enough.

Anna and Simon rode in silence the forty-minute distance to the agency's extra apartment where Simon brought the SUV to a stop along the curb in front of the entrance.

"Any idea where we go from here?" Simon asked as Anna looked blankly out of the front window.

"Not a clue. I think we should focus on notifying William's family and getting a funeral arranged. Another one," Anna said shaking her head in disbelief. She couldn't believe that William was gone. For real this time.

"Do you want me to do it?" Simon asked, "Contact William's family that is."

"No. I was really close to William. He was more of an uncle to me, and after my father died, he watched over me like a father. I think I owe it to him," Anna opened the door of the SUV and stepped onto the curb. She closed the door behind her and swung her bag over her shoulder. She rested her hand on the door, and through the open window, she thanked Simon and told him she would call him when she was ready.

Simon waited until the front door of the apartment building closed shut behind her before he began to pull away from the curb. The whole way home he kept replaying the events of the day in his mind and he couldn't help but think this wasn't over, but he also was confused about how to continue without William. He decided to give Anna some time before he began to pursue the investigation. Until then he needed to inform the rest of the team that William was dead. And that was something he wasn't looking forward to doing.

Anna was running the same thoughts through her mind as she walked through the apartment. There was so much to consider, and she wasn't sure that the whole ring with Quantum would end with Ashbury's death, but she had to try. She just wasn't sure she was going to have the energy or drive to finish. Especially with the realization that she was probably able to trust Simon more than Denis at this point.

She just couldn't believe that William was gone, Denis was probably a double agent, and that a high-ranking representative of the Executive Branch of the government was behind the explosion that killed so many of Anna's friends and coworkers. And ultimately led her to leave the agency altogether.

But for now, she knew she had to deal with William's family. She forced herself to face William's death and his family and she pulled her phone from her pocket. She opened her contacts and scrolled through until she came to the name she was looking for. She pressed the phone number and tilted her head back as the phone began to ring on the other end.

She hoped he would pick up, she wasn't sure if she was going to have the strength to try and make a call a second time.

On the third ring, his deep voice greeted her with a cheerful tone. "Anna! What a surprise. How are you?"

Anna closed her eyes, "CJ, I have some news. It's about your father. You may want to sit down."

CHAPTER 23-

CJ decided a private service was the best way to deal with laying his father to rest since everyone else thought he was already dead. CJ was the last relative that was still alive, and as it turned out, he was aware of what William was doing. He knew that his father was running a secret operation and that he didn't die in the explosion that everyone thought prematurely claimed his life.

CJ and William had set up an alias email account and communicated through draft emails they would leave in limbo in the account. They would never send any of them, meaning that they couldn't be traced. They would each log in and read the draft the other had written and then would delete the text and write their response. Simple but effective.

Anna was glad that CJ knew William was alive and that he didn't have to go through the pain of losing him twice. CJ told Anna he felt as if he was part of his secret operation when they left their messages in the email account, he knew that his father loved being an agent and he couldn't live with letting his country be ruined by a crooked politician, so as hard as it was to stay quiet, CJ knew how important it was to his father.

Anna now stood at the edge of William's grave holding a bouquet that she bought earlier in the day and was now beginning to wilt under the heat of the sun. CJ thought it would be less confusing if they used the grave marker that they set for the false funeral after the explosion. Anna knew it made sense, however, it was odd standing at the same gravesite twice for the same person.

It was just CJ and Anna at the funeral, and neither of them felt a need to speak. After William was laid to rest, CJ kissed Anna goodbye and made her promise to call him soon.

A breeze wove through the headstones and roused Anna from her trance. She realized she had been standing in the same spot and twenty minutes had passed without notice. She laid the flowers she was holding onto the fresh mound of soil and then placed her hand flat against the ground.

"Thank you, William. You gave me a chance to say goodbye the best way we knew how," Anna wiped the tears from her eyes and returned to her car.

On the way to her car she knew she would pass by her father's grave and wasn't sure that she would have the strength, or courage, to visit it today. However, she soon found herself standing in front of his resting spot reading the inscription under his name and the dates engraved into the stone.

'Honour belongs to those who never forsake the truth.'

Anna was sure it was something her father attributed to Nelson Mandela, who was a hero of his. No matter who said it, it suited her father perfectly.

Anna sat for a while cleaning the weeds around the base of the grave and dusted off the pollen that had accumulated on the top of the headstone. The benefit of a family member being buried in a government cemetery is that it is extremely well-manicured, so no one laid to rest ever looks as if they had been forgotten. Even if their families never came.

She was exhausted. The last couple of years had taken their toll on her and Anna wasn't sure she would have the desire or energy to continue. She walked past rows of headstones and over graves that curved around trees and flowed over undulating hills as the lawn neared the riverbank.

The dates that were etched into the stones told only a fraction of the story about the souls that lay underneath. Anna grew to learn that there were always many layers for each story told, and it may take a lifetime to understand the ones that were close to us, let alone the people we only peripherally knew.

Her thoughts turned to Denis, whose grave was just a few rows from where she was walking. She was struck by the irony that he would be the second person whose grave was filled with someone other than the name etched on the headstone above the ground. Her emotions went from sadness to anger as she reeled from thinking about William's sacrifice to Denis's betrayal. Anna began to head toward the location of Denis's grave when she decided that the day belonged to William and she changed her path and began to walk back to where she parked.

Anna saw the bright yellow Mustang before she saw Simon leaning against it. He had parked next to her car and he stood dressed in black slacks and shirt as if he had intended on joining them at William's gravesite.

"Not exactly the car of an undercover agent," Anna said as she pointed to the bright yellow car Simon was leaning against.

"No, I guess not," Simon chuckled. "How did it go?"

Anna shrugged her shoulders, "My second funeral for William, and I still can't believe he is gone."

Simon pushed his body away from the side of his car and slipped his hands into his pockets as he walked toward Anna, "Neither can I. William saved my life, more ways than you could know. I'm glad I had a chance to repay him. But there's still a lot we need to do before we can lay this to rest."

Anna shook her head, "I don't think so Simon. I'm not even sure I have what it takes to be successful as an agent anymore."

A look of shock fell over Simon's face. "What are you talking about?"

"I can't do this anymore Simon," Anna slammed her hands on the roof of her car and looked at Simon. "I will just be second-guessing myself from this point on, and that won't make me a good agent."

"What are you talking about? There is no tougher, surer agent I have ever worked with," Simon leaned in, so he could make his point without yelling.

"That was then, Simon. Now with everything that has happened over the last few weeks, I feel like everything I based my whole truth or knowledge about the people in my life has crumbled. My dad's involvement with the Latvian agent left behind, William's secret investigation and death, Denis being some sort of crazy double agent, and you!" Anna's voice was shaking.

"Yeah, and me!" Simon threw his hands up.

"You know what I mean," Anna explained. "People I thought I could trust I can't and when I thought I couldn't trust you I . . ." Anna's voice trailed off.

"You what?" Simon asked, wanting her to finish.

"I feel like you are one of the few people I can fully trust," Anna felt a tear rolling down her cheek and she quickly wiped it away.

Simon smiled, "I knew I was growing on you again."

They both laughed.

"I don't know Simon. I just don't think I have the fire in me anymore," Anna concluded.

"Then take a look at this and see what you think," Simon reached in through the open window of his car and pulled out a copy of the morning paper. On the front page was a picture of Ashbury that was taken on the day he was being given an award by a group of young campers for the work he did helping them raise money during a summer fundraising campaign. Above the photo, the caption read: "Altruistic Senator Dies of Heart Attack"

The story was not one that Anna needed to take the time to read. She was used to the same political cover-up, whitewashing jargon. Instead of Ashbury's illegal dealings with enemies of the country, he was lauded as a local hero and a great progressive mind in the government.

Anna held the paper in her hands and shook her head, "Can't say that I'm surprised. Disappointed but not surprised."

Simon pointed to the article below the article on Ashbury's life and untimely death. "Keep reading."

Anna glanced at the article below that she would have missed if Simon had not pointed it out to her. "They're going ahead with the State Dinner. It says here it was Ashbury's project and to honor him they are going to see his plans completed."

"We both know what that could mean. More backroom deals for Quantum," Simon said.

"So, what exactly can we do about it?" Anna folded the paper and handed it back to Simon who tossed it back through the same window he extracted it from just moments ago.

"Look, even though to the public Ashbury's death is being made out to be just a plain old heart attack, the government knows what he has been up to all along. It's a little odd that they would still be going along with the dinner knowing what Ashbury had going on behind the scenes with some of the diplomats that are attending.

"Agreed," Anna said with her arms crossed over her chest. She just wanted to be home already, but she could feel herself slowly slipping back into Simon's plan.

"I figured that could only mean one thing," Simon said, not finishing his sentence knowing that Anna would want to weigh in on the topic.

"It means that there's someone else in the government that's involved with Quantum," Anna said.

"Someone of importance could only pull this off right after we blew Ashbury's cover," Simon said.

"What do you think we should do?" Anna asked.

"We need to find out who that someone was and get to them before they get to us," Simon slapped his hands together and waited for Anna's response.

"We'll need some help," Anna said.

"I was thinking the same thing and I already contacted Alastair. He is digging as we speak," Simon said proudly.

"He took your call?" Anna asked, only half-jokingly.

"Apparently saving your life counts for something with him," Simon said.

Anna could feel the blush rise in her cheeks. She shook the feeling off and told Simon to meet at the apartment in a half hour and they would get started.

Anna waited and watched as Simon slid behind the wheel of the bright yellow power car and drove slowly out of the cemetery along the narrow path toward the iron gates.

Anna thought once more about walking over to Denis's grave before she finally abandoned the idea and got into her car and left the cemetery through the same gate that Simon did.

Two rows away a man walked out from behind a line of trees and made his way toward the same grave that Anna contemplated visiting. He knelt and placed three flowers at the base of the headstone and dropped his head in contemplative reflection and he rested his right hand on the top of the headstone. The muffled cell phone buzzing came from the inside pocket of his jacket and stirred his attention. He pulled out the phone and raised the phone to his ear.

"Yes, I saw the dinner is still planned," he answered the caller. "We'll stick to our original schedule."

He listened while the caller gave him the final instructions.

"Yes, I'll be careful." He reassured the caller. "I love you too."

The man then disconnected the call and turned to leave the cemetery. As he walked away, he wiped the tears from his eyes, knowing he was leaving behind his brother, that lay below the surface in a grave marked with his name.

CHAPTER 24-

Simon arrived approximately twenty minutes after Anna returned to the apartment. She knew it was better to not have gone to Denis's grave, especially since he wasn't even buried there. But she couldn't brush away the feeling that she should have gone.

Anna was halfway through her second cup of coffee when the door buzzer rang. She buzzed him in, showed him toward the coffee, and then they sat at the dining room table with the multitude of papers scattered around the surface. She attempted to organize them chronologically, then when that didn't seem to make sense, she organized them according to their regions. That also didn't seem to make the situation any clearer.

"Look, we have a lot of information to work with. Let's just piece it together one step at a time again," Simon said.

"Okay, let's start with the letter that Josh received from his girlfriend. That is the first time an outsider saw any pattern that pointed toward Quantum," Anna suggested. She remembered whenever the team hit a roadblock that William always suggested to go back to the beginning and try and look at the same situation with new eyes.

"Good idea," Simon began to sort through the pile of papers and pulled out the copy of the letter that Josh received from Sonja. "How did Josh's girlfriend get this information again?"

"She was completing some research for her doctorate for her economics degree. Her thesis focused on something to do with international corporate ownership. She had just pulled corporations registered in various countries around the world and she spotted some inconsistencies. She wasn't even looking for them," Anna was remembering the report William had given her regarding Josh's girlfriend's death and felt she also now owed it to her to keep going.

Anna continued to explain, "Sonja also happened to be a law major and she recognized a lot of the dates for the registrations for these companies had coincided with changes in government policies for tariffs, civil wars, and even refugee policies. It didn't seem like much at first, but she noticed a few of the executives in the corporations were also heads of state. So, she passed the information along to Josh."

"Then she was killed," Simon stated.

"Yes, then she was killed," Anna said.

Anna walked over to the whiteboard and taped the letter Sonja had sent to Josh right before she was killed. Underneath, she taped a picture of Josh and beside his picture, she wrote some notes in point form.

"Josh worked for Quantum undercover posing as a numbers guy, and we have to assume he also was successful at hiding many accounts and companies to keep his cover safe. While working for Quantum he also tracked a key Russian company whose board was made up of Russian government officials."

"That is why Josh was at the Abramovich wedding. I wonder what he was trying to do there?" Simon said.

"All this information made it back to William, except for what he uncovered about Blackwater," Anna wrote Blackwater in full caps on the right side of the board with a question mark beside it.

"The last thing he said to do was to follow the money," Simon recounted.

Anna then taped the copy of the bank account numbers under Josh's name and drew a line connecting them. "Yes, and that took us to Riga where we, eventually, figured out the account numbers and deposits were coded for where the agents would meet in secret. Face to face so there was no trace of the conversation."

Simon walked over to the board and to the right of the bank statements he taped a picture of Logan James, "And let's not forget your friend from the cemetery, Logan. He was one of the agents making the deposits."

"And he also was purchasing a vial from Dr. Petrov when I followed him to Riga. Just before he was killed." Anna said.

"By Denis," Simon stated.

Anna still had a hard time with that fact and chose to not respond to Simon's comment, "Logan was able to disguise each trip to Riga with a government relations trip so none of his trips were ever questioned and he made it through security in each country without much scrutiny."

"Okay. So, Sonja is dead. Josh is dead. Logan is dead. And Denis is probably alive," Anna said as she put a bright red x beside the names or pictures taped to the board.

"That brings us to the explosion. This is where Ashbury makes an appearance," Simon taped a picture of Ashbury to the board and drew a line to Logan and Josh. He stood back and looked at the board and then drew a line with a question mark to Denis. "We still aren't sure how Denis is connected in this."

"No, you're right," Anna added. "We know the explosion was set because William was getting too close to uncovering what Ashbury was doing. That, Ashbury confirmed for us before he died."

"But do you think Denis knew about the explosion?" Simon asked. "I just don't see that."

"No, neither do I. No matter what Denis was up to, his brother died in that explosion. And I can't believe that he would have let all those innocent people die in that building," Anna turned to face Simon. "I saw how he was with each person in that office. There's no way that he would have wanted them to die."

Simon agreed.

"Okay, where does that leave us with Denis?" Anna finally asked, addressing the elephant in the room.

Simon was the one to write under Denis's picture, "Brother and sister, brother is dead, and we don't know where the sister is. Parents are also dead, but we also know his father was a spy for our government, and we left him there to suffer under the next government."

"And the siblings were split up. Denis went to Britain, and brother and sister joined a rebel group," Anna said. "Maybe that's where the difference is."

Simon crossed his arms in front of his chest, "What do you mean?"

"Well, for Ashbury it was all business. Crooked business, but business. It was all about money for him and his corporation. But for Denis and his siblings, it was personal," Anna explained.

"Then how do you explain his sister becoming one of the agents involved with Ashbury. Remember she was making some of the deposits for a while," Simon said.

Anna paused for a moment then added, "Maybe that was part of their plan. Maybe that was her way in."

Simon nodded, "That leaves us with everyone who is involved with is dead, except Denis and his sister."

"And Ashbury's operation was too big to die with him. Remember his family began as security and transportation a couple of generations ago. Quantum and all the subsidiaries are large enough to run without him. And in any event, there would always be a contingency plan in place should a major player die," Anna said. "I don't even know if we could stop it if we wanted to."

"Do you think there is any relevance to the number of utility companies that Quantum owns through subsidiaries?" Simon asked.

"I am sure there is, I just don't see it now," Anna said.

The sound of a knock on the apartment door diverted Simon and Anna from their focus on the whiteboard in front of them.

Anna walked to the door and unlatched the lock as she turned the handle and pulled the door open, as she gasped at the six-foot-tall man standing in front of her.

CHAPTER 25-

"Alastair!" Anna shouted. She threw her arms around his neck as he stood perched at the entrance to the apartment with each arm weighed down with heavy equipment cases and a large canvas rucksack strapped to his back.

"How about you ask me in?" Alastair's accent always calmed Anna and she realized tears were falling from her eyes.

"I am so happy to see you! But why are you here?" Anna stepped back into the apartment and held the door wide open so Alastair could step inside with the large load of baggage he was carrying.

Alastair dropped the heavy cases to the floor and pointed toward Simon, "He called me. Thought you could use me here."

Anna blushed as she glanced at Simon, "Thank you, Simon. Alastair is exactly what I need."

Simon interjected, "He's what we need actually." Simon extended his hand to Alastair. "Thanks for coming so quickly."

Alastair hesitated slightly, then took Simon's hand, "Not a problem. Seems like you're a little gutted right now."

"We're what?" Simon was never to keep up or understand Alastair's British slang.

"Despair. Trouble," Anna translated for Simon.

Alastair tossed his rucksack in the corner of the room and hoisted his two cases onto the table. He quickly unlatched the cases and in a matter of minutes had a portable research station ready to go.

"Where are you right now?" Alastair pointed to the whiteboard referencing the photos, documents, and Anna and Simon's writing in marker.

Simon waved his hand across the board and said, "Except for Denis and his sister, Eloria, everyone is dead."

"Lovely, not much to go on," Alastair said.

"I was thinking," Anna said, "That, possibly, the situation with Denis and his sister isn't as tightly connected with Ashbury and Quantum as we may have initially thought."

"I agree. The situation with Denis seems too personal. Quantum is a money machine," Alastair said as he typed away at his computer bringing the screen to life.

"I also think Ashbury must have someone else on the inside. Up high in the government," Anna said.

"Why?" Simon asked.

"Why else would the state dinner be going ahead as planned. Someone was able to convince the President to go ahead with the state dinner even with everything that we uncovered. You would think something like uncovering Ashbury using his government connections to run Quantum, and implicating the government in the process, would be enough to put the brakes on anything he was working on," Anna said.

"Unless there were more fingers in the pot," Simon said.

"Exactly what I was thinking," Alastair finished. "There are two tracks of information here. Ashbury and whomever he may have connections with, and Denis and whatever his plans are." Alastair pointed to the screen on his computer and while Anna and Simon began to read it, he tapped away at the second computer and brought the second series of information up on the screen.

"Are these all of Ashbury's holdings?" Anna asked.

"Everything. Personal and business. I was able to pull every one of Quantum's subsidiaries. There were almost two hundred. I listed the countries and board members. I highlighted the board members that also have government postings," Alastair explained.

"Every company has a government official on the board." Simon noticed.

"So much for tight regulations," Alastair said. "I also pulled Quantum's regulations outlining who should take over if Ashbury is unable to continue his duties."

"Mitch McCallum. The Secretary of Defence?" Anna said.

"Mitch McCallum junior. The Secretary of Defence's son. Still, a little too close to be a coincidence," Alastair said.

"So that is how they probably were able to convince the President to not cancel the dinner," Simon said.

"I set a program to run through the event organizer's email for when she will be away at a lunch appointment. The system is set to indicate if more than one person is accessing information in any of the emails at one time," Alastair said.

"How do you know she won't check her email?" Anna asked.

"Her appointment is with her dentist. I hacked the dentist's office files and changed her file to indicate a higher dosage of novocaine for her procedure," Alastair grinned.

"What do you hope to find?" Simon asked.

"Well for starters, we can hopefully trace the emails back to whoever pushed for the dinner to go ahead. Then we can go from there," Alastair said.

Anna was looking at the second computer, "This is about Denis and Eloria."

Alastair swung his body around to face the second computer, "Yes, I found a few interesting things about your co-worker."

"Give us the short version," Simon said.

"Not sure there is one. You already know about Denis's parents dying and he and his siblings being separated. Denis was adopted by a British couple and by all accounts had a great upbringing. He had the best of everything, including a University education at Cambridge. However, his adoptive parents thought it would be best if he never had contact with either of his siblings. They thought it would make for an easier transition."

"A bit harsh, don't you think? Considering what they went through," Simon said.

"Getting soft Simon?" Anna asked.

"Well, it seems as if Denis didn't worry too much about what his adoptive parents thought because it appears that he was in contact with both his brother and sister over the years," Alastair said. "I spoke with an old roommate of Denis's from Cambridge, and he remembers two family members visiting. He couldn't be sure if they were cousins or siblings. He remembered walking in once when they were visiting and caught them speaking an eastern European language. Possibly Latvian, now that we know where they were from. They stopped speaking and the roommate thought they looked suspicious. Denis got angry and said to never interrupt him. It was the first, and last, time that his roommate ever saw Denis angry or lash out. That is why it stuck in his memory. They never spoke of it again."

"Well, so we know they were in contact. What does that tell us about what they were doing?" Anna asked.

"I was able to trace his brother to a rebel sect he joined that was active in Latvia, Russia, and Serbia. With so much turmoil in the region, the UN had been tracking the number of offshoot groups. They often would go from seemingly peaceful protesters to violent rebels depending on the change in government. At some point, the UN had lost track of him and thought he may even be dead. But we now know he wasn't."

"And Eloria?" Anna asked.

"Eloria joined the same group as Oskar did. She was peripherally involved. Somewhere along the line, Quantum got involved in the region and began to infiltrate the smaller rebel groups to try and get them on their side in the event they needed them to stir up trouble to alter the value of the goods they were trading. Eloria was part of one of the smaller groups Quantum approached and eventually she became a trusted agent making the deposits that were used as code messages."

"Does she still work for Quantum?" Simon asked.

"She doesn't appear to. When she was part of the rebel group part of her cover was her job as a model. She would fly to different regions under the guise of being on a photoshoot but around the same time that she stopped making deposits for Quantum she seemed to ramp up her work as an international model. There is a record of her moving to England where she worked for a modeling agency in London, which was at the same time that Denis was training in your agency. She was able to travel between countries without much notice because of her job as a model and eventually was offered a job at a New York agency," Alastair pulled up some photos of Eloria from her modeling days. "She took it and moved there a short while later."

Anna was transfixed on the photos that Alastair had found of Eloria. She couldn't shake the feeling that she knew her from somewhere.

"And does she still work as a model there?" Simon asked.

"No. The typical American dream. Moved to New York, applied for citizenship, and then changed her name," Alastair said. "then she met an up and coming Senator, fell madly in love and they married."

Anna shouted, "I know who she is!"

"Who did she marry?" Simon asked at the same moment that Anna had made her revelation.

"His name was Senator Harris J. Sanderson," Alastair announced.

"You mean President Sanderson?" Simon asked.

"Then that means," Simon trailed off.

"Denis's sister is the First Lady," Anna said.

CHAPTER 26–

Anna had slumped into the chair that was in front of the second computer that displayed the information on Denis's sister, Eloria. The First Lady.

"This is big guys," Anna said. "How exactly are we going to tackle this?"

"The same way we tackle everything," Simon knelt beside Anna. "How would you approach this if it wasn't the First Lady?"

Anna contemplated Simon's question, "I would find a way in to confront her and stop whatever it was she was up to."

"Then that's what we'll do," Simon said.

"I can hack into her assistant's email and see what pops up," Alastair suggested, but he was typing away before either Simon or Anna could answer.

The alarm sound was like that of a bus in reverse, but it was coming from Alastair's first computer.

"Whoa! We got a hit!" Alastair announced as he swung around to give his full attention to the first computer.

He silenced the alarm and opened the blinking app in the bottom corner of the screen.

"An alert for what?" Anna said as she and Simon moved closer to the screen.

"The bank account in Riga. I almost forgot about it. I figured with you two confronting Ashbury that they would have gone silent. It appears that our friends are unaware of our knowledge of their routine," Alastair brought up the details of the most recent deposit to the account in Riga.

"It's account number 4775 11120 7401," Alastair read out loud.

"That's Washington," Anna said.

"The deposits are: $10.29, $1,300 and $7,717." Alastair listed the deposits as Anna calculated the numbers and what they referred to.

"That is the day of the state dinner at one in the afternoon," Anna calculated.

The three looked at each other and knew they were simultaneously thinking the same thought.

"Where are they meeting?" Anna was the one to say it out loud.

"Maybe we can cross-reference some numbers," Alastair enlarged the screen that was downloading the event coordinator's email and calendar and went to work. In a matter of moments pages with highlighted text began to appear across the screen as his program scanned the event coordinator's email for any reference that matched the same digits in the deposit.

"There's an appointment booked in the hotel that the state dinner is being held at. Look at the room number," Alastair said.

"7717." Anna read the numbers and knew that it was too much of a coincidence.

"It could be a trap," Simon suggested. "It's what I would do."

"It could be," Alastair concurred. "Or they could be pushing through the agenda because it is too important to wait just because Ashbury died."

"We need to be there at the meeting to find out who is meeting and why. I think I can get into the room earlier and set a couple of those fancy bugs of yours that no one can trace Alastair," Simon stepped away from the desk to make a call to a contact of his at the same hotel.

As Simon was engaged in his phone call Anna was focusing on the information Alastair revealed about Eloria, "What could she possibly have been planning with Denis?"

"You don't have any idea? You sure you don't remember anything that Denis was particularly focused on during the time you knew him, and you trained together?" Alastair asked.

"Nothing. And believe me, I have strained my thinking to come up with one shred of evidence. Something that would make sense of any of this. Denis was my partner, we depended upon each other for our lives. I just can't believe everything I thought about him was a lie," Anna was emotionally exhausted, but she knew she had to see this to the end. Especially with the information that came to light about Eloria.

Alastair turned his attention to the second computer and began to review the scanned emails that came from the First Lady's assistant's email account.

"This is interesting. Many emails are going between the First Lady's assistant and the President's assistant on the evening of Ashbury's death," Simon noted.

"What are they about?" Anna asked.

"The state dinner," Alastair said. "It seems the President's office was planning on canceling it until the First Lady pressured him to keep it as planned."

"I would have been sure it was McCallum's office that pressured him to keep it as scheduled. Why would the First Lady have been involved?" Anna asked.

"Seems as if she felt it was in the best interest of diplomacy, even though they were aware of Asbury's illegal dealings," Alastair said. "All in all, there were close to forty emails between them."

Alastair paused then asked Anna, "Don't you think that is a bit strange?"

Anna looked at Alastair, "Which one? Eloria pushing for the dinner or the number of emails?"

"Wouldn't you just call your husband if you wanted to convince him to do something? Why would you have your assistant email his assistant? They may be in the White House, but they are still a married couple."

"Doesn't mean they are happy though," Anna said.

Simon was finished his call and was slipping his phone into his back pocket when he returned to where Anna and Alastair were sitting, "Okay, my guy can get me in with the food delivery trucks, but that means I have to leave now. Do you have any of those fancy bugs Alastair?" Simon held out his hand.

Alastair slid his hand into the back part of his computer case and extracted a small bag and handed them to Simon, "I'll activate them as soon as you leave."

"Thanks," Simon began to walk toward the door but stopped and put his hand on Anna's shoulder, "We'll figure this one out soon."

Alastair watched Anna's face blush as Simon walked out of the apartment.

"I really think he has changed Anna," Alastair said. "And I think he genuinely cares about what happens to you."

Anna shook off Alastair's comment and returned to the emails that she and Alastair were examining. But in the back of her mind, Anna was thinking that she was beginning to care about Simon as well.

CHAPTER 27-

Simon arrived at the hotel and waited in the back lane as Chris had instructed him to do. As the extended delivery truck approached the loading dock, Simon walked alongside it and jumped up onto the landing dock just as the driver put the truck into park.

By the time the driver stepped out of his cab and made his way to the back of the truck Simon was waiting to help unload it. When the employees of the hotel heard the truck arrive, they walked out onto the loading dock to meet the delivery and saw both Simon and the driver waiting for them.

For Simon, it was perfect timing. The driver thought he was with the hotel, and the hotel thought he was with the driver. No one questioned his being there.

They quickly worked to unload the enormous crates of prepared and raw food, and Simon busied himself near the freezer and when he was sure he was out of anyone's line of sight, he made his way to the back hall and toward the staff room. Simon grabbed a staff uniform and slipped into a back room to change.

On his way to the elevator, Simon grabbed an order that was waiting to be taken up to a guest for room service. He arrived at the floor that the meeting room was situated and easily worked his way down the hall and into the room without being noticed.

Just as promised, Chris had left a room key on top of the emergency fire alarm where it was out of the light of sight for anyone that may have walked by it in the hall. With a quick swipe, the room lock changed from red to green and the door opened with ease and Simon was inside.

He locked the door and placed three of the bugs around the room. He positioned them so no matter where anyone was speaking, they would be able to pick up the conversation clearly. He didn't want to leave anything to chance. The room was a little larger than a standard hotel room and contained only couches and chairs intended for formal meetings and not sleeping. Simon was prepared that the room was more than likely going to be swept for bugs, so knowing that the units Alastair designed would not trigger an alarm, he was willing to take more of a risk to get the bugs closer to the seating area.

After Simon had placed the units where he wanted them, he picked up the tray and left the room. As he was making his way to the elevator, he began to discard the tray in front of a guest's room door. He noticed on a server's trolley there was a tray with a note. He looked down at the note and realized the tray indicated the meal was for Mikhail Ivanov. Mikhail Ivanov was the Russian diplomat's son who was traveling with him to Washington on this trip and his name jumped out for Simon because he was well known to government agencies for how he was able to get himself in (and then out) of trouble seamlessly. He had been accused of everything from DUIs to assault but flaunted his ability to avoid charges because of his diplomatic protection. Ivanov also had a propensity to party heavily and would often be overheard bragging about his father's connections and meetings. Simon thought he may as well take advantage of the opportunity and decided to place a set of ears in his room. Simon pulled out a bug and affixed it to the inside bottom of the container that was overflowing with white and pink sugar packs. He made sure the paper packs covered the bug and then pressed the floor that would take him to Ivanov's room.

CHAPTER 28–

Anna was tapping her finger on her chin trying to force herself to think of a way to get into speak with Eloria, or Mary Sanderson which is how the world knew her.

"Can you send a masked email to Eloria's assistant?" Anna asked although she knew the answer would be yes.

"Who do you want it to come from?" Alastair asked.

"The seamstress who is working on the First Lady's dress. Change the time that the dress is being delivered. Move it up so I can show up in place of the dressmaker, and that way I should be able to get in without any credentials," Anna suggested.

"Good idea. I can have any emails that Eloria's assistant sends out to reroute to me so the seamstress will be none the wiser." Alastair got to work finding the contact information for the seamstress and creating the email that would hopefully deceive the First Lady and her assistant. Alastair hit send, "Now we wait for a response."

As Anna had suspected Eloria's assistant always had her phone on her and probably still feeling the effects of the additional novocaine typed away her response confirming the early delivery of the dress. She instructed Anna to come to the side entrance and ask for Jane as she would be busy preparing for the guests that evening.

"Perfect. I'll be able to get in tomorrow and finally confront Eloria." Anna was nervous about coming face to face with Denis's sister. She had so many questions, the first she wanted to ask was about Denis?

"While we are waiting for Simon to return, what else did you find out about Eloria? I want to be prepared when I confront her," Anna said.

Alastair opened the research document he had on Eloria. "Well, in addition to being beautiful she is no dope either. She has a degree in Chemistry she received while at the University of Latvia. She was a straight–A student and can speak four languages fluently."

Anna remembered that Denis also could speak many languages. She wondered what else Eloria and Denis had in common. Anna secretly wondered if she would have also been a close friend of hers had the situation been different.

Then Anna sat up straight, "Did you say a chemistry degree?"

"Yeah, why?" Alastair asked.

Anna shook her head slightly, "I am not sure. Probably nothing."

Alastair crossed his arms in front of his chest, "Come on."

"Remember Dr. Petrov? Denis grabbed the vial Logan got from him. I was just wondering if the two were connected," Anna said.

Alastair refocused on the computer screen, "Who knows, but we have something more immediate to focus on. Like figuring out why it was so important to have this dinner go ahead after Ashbury was killed."

"What else does Eloria talk about during her emails with her husband regarding the state dinner? Or more pointedly, who else does she mention?" Anna asked.

Alastair began to type away on his keyboard and entered a search sequence that highlighted names of individuals that may have been mentioned during the string of emails that were traveling between the two on the night of Ashbury's death.

"It looks as though there is some focus on the Russian diplomat, Boris Ivanov. The President's office is arranging a meeting with him before dinner. Or his wife seems to have subtly arranged it," Alastair was scanning the emails and a smile began to creep across his face. "She's good. Look here. The way she mentions him meeting with Ivanov you can tell it is her idea."

"But in the end, it looks like the President himself arranged the meeting. I wonder what that's all about?" Anna asked.

"Seems to be under the guise of trade," Alastair noted.

Anna looked slyly at Alastair, "Is there any way you can get in to see Ivanov's emails?"

Alastair raised his eyebrows, "That may be a bit tricky." Then he smiled, "But yes. It will take a while, the Russians are pros at hacking and email security."

"Great. Let's see what else Ivanov has planned while he is here in Washington," Anna stretched her arms over her head, and she felt an instant release of tension in the back of her shoulders.

Anna left Alastair to his email hacking and walked to the kitchen and began to get them each a cold drink. She knew Alastair well enough to know what he would want to drink and didn't feel the need to ask him. Anna grabbed the two chilled glasses and made her way back to where Alastair was sitting. The intense look of excitement was evident in Alastair's expression as he challenged himself with the labyrinth of security measures the Russian's had put in place.

Anna could have sworn she heard Alastair mumble, "Brilliant!" under his breath as he tapped away at his keyboard with delight.

Simon hurriedly entered the apartment, slamming the door behind him. He tossed the small bag with the remaining bugs on the table next to Alastair and rested his hand on his shoulder.

"Looks like we have two targets at the hotel," Simon announced. "I placed some of those beauties in the room that we think the secret meeting is taking place, aaaaand," with a slight but dramatic pause. "I happened to come across an opportunity to place one of Alastair's devices in Mikhail Ivanov's room."

"How did you get into his room? And how did you even know he was there?" Anna said. Every agent was aware of who Ivanov was because of his illegal and shady dealings that he openly flaunted because of the protection that diplomatic immunity afforded him.

"Well, I was able to place it on a tray going into his room," Simon looked directly at Alastair. "Please tell me you activated the bugs?"

Alastair nodded, "I have it on an automatic record. I triggered them when you left the apartment."

Simon slapped Alastair on the back, something Alastair detested, but he did his best to ignore, "You're brilliant Alastair!" Simon exclaimed.

"I know," Alastair responded and shifted in his seat moving away from Simon's frat-house approval.

Alastair began to play the sound-activated recording that triggered when Ivanov began to eat the late breakfast that was delivered to his room. The first ten minutes were sounds of Mikhail slurping his coffee and eating the eggs benedict he ordered with a double side of bacon. The sound of his swallows and chewing were interrupted by a knock on the door.

Mikhail had answered the door and after a brief greeting in Russian, the visitor began to speak English, indicating that Russian was not his first language. And judging by the accented English he was speaking, neither was English. The two spent little time on pleasantries and began to speak immediately of Ashbury and his death. The two revealed through their discussion that they believed his death to be as was reported to the public – due to a heart condition.

"That would explain why the routine of using the bank deposits as the code wasn't interrupted. They don't suspect a thing," Anna said.

The two began to speak about a recent tariff that was going to be placed on the Syrian government's purchase of refinery equipment. Keeping the price of oil production high for them but not attracting attention as an oil ban.

It became evident the man that Ivanov was meeting with was Syrian and the two were making plans to sell a cheaper version of the equipment through Russian channels, avoiding the U.S. tariffs and forcing the profit from the sale into their pockets because of their ownership in the Russian company.

Mikhail Ivanov was cocky and brazen in his conversation with the Syrian, "I've been able to work both sides of the deal perfectly and I convinced my father to pressure Ashbury to apply the tariff just as your companies were preparing to purchase a new round of equipment. Thankfully, he was able to complete his business with Ashbury before his death."

It was the Syrian's turn to speak, "And are we still agreed that all additional financial transactions are to go through the company Quantum set up?"

"Yes, yes, there is no problem. It'll all go as planned," Mikhail assured the Syrian.

"And how did you convince your father to pressure Ashbury?" The Syrian asked.

Ivanov laughed, "We all have secrets, my friend. And even some Russian ones are too dark to reveal."

The Syrian left the room and Ivanov finished his meal and then once they heard the shower in the bathroom, Alastair stopped the recording and turned his chair to face Anna and Simon.

"Seems like propitious timing that you came across Ivanov's tray," Alastair said.

"It's interesting, but it doesn't help us sort out what is happening at the state dinner," Anna spoke but the other two were thinking the same thing.

"What about Ivanov's secret? Any idea what that is about?" Simon asked Alastair.

Alastair needed no prompting and quickly began to run a back search on the senior, Boris Ivanov.

The breadth and scope of Alastair's search capabilities went way beyond a typical web search. Even key top-level researchers that Anna had worked with at the agency were unable to come close to the extent or the effectiveness that Alastair's searches did. Anna learned over time that there were only two key rules. Never to ask where Alastair found his information or if he was sure about what he found.

Diving into hidden files and back drawer level emails, Alastair was able to uncover little about Ivanov that was remotely illegal until he reached back to a time when he was a Russian officer on patrol in a remote Latvian village. It was during a point in Ivanov's career that he was trying to make a name for himself and impress upon those in charge that he was the go-to man for any operation. He was known for his toughness and extreme harshness against anything that wasn't Russian. His approach to disobedience was feared among those living in the village that he controlled, and he was revered among those who worked for him.

Court documents showed the young Russian officer was accused of terrorizing the people in the small village and he was suspected of many attacks against women and children while on patrol in the village. When Latvia began to struggle free from Soviet rule, many villagers came forward to level accusations against certain officers one being Ivanov. At the beginning of his trial, many of the women who came forward with accusations against him had either gone missing or turned up dead. It didn't take long after that for any remaining accusers to back away from their claim claiming poor memory or the effects of traumatic stress causing them to accuse the wrong man.

Ivanov was set free and returned to service in the Russian government, this time with more honors beside his name.

Among the women who came forward to accuse Ivanov was Inga Evanishyn, Denis and Eloria's mother.

"I can only imagine how abandoned Andris would have felt. Not only was he counting on the American government to get his family safely out of Latvia but because he was left there, his wife was abused," Even though Anna disagreed with things that Denis's was accused of doing she could see how the events of his past set the path he, Oskar and Eloria would take for the rest of their lives.

"I think I can guess as to what the First Lady's interest in the state dinner is," Simon suggested.

"She must be planning to kill Ivanov," and Anna began to wonder if she even wanted to stop it from happening.

CHAPTER 29-

Preparing for the state dinner was a task Anna was learning was no small feat. When reviewing the plethora of e-mails that covered everything from the intense security procedures to be put in place right down to the appropriate color of flowers – to ensure important guests were not offended. It became evident that there were possibly more people involved behind the scenes than attending the dinner.

Anna had determined that no matter what plan Eloria had intended to carry out, she had taken an oath to defend her country, or at least what was good about it.

Anna grabbed the brushed steel handle and pulled the folding wooden closet door open revealing a closet jammed with clothes that were stocked for whatever agents happened to be staying at the apartment. The assortment covered everything from formal wear to clothes that would suffice as utility worker's gear. In the back of the closet hung a garment bag with bright pink material showing through the plastic window on the bag. Anna pulled the bag close enough to unzip it and as she pulled back the vinyl, she saw the full view of the shiny dress that could only have been intended for a disguise as a bridesmaid. Anna knew this dress was expendable and had wondered why it hadn't been thrown out earlier. She pulled the zipper up closing the garment bag and then with a push of her right hand, closed the closet door.

Anna changed into a pair of black pants and pulled on a non-descript white shirt and then slipped her feet into her favorite black loafers. She knew she had to look as plain and simple as possible and wanted to avoid any facial recognition security software that may be in place before the event. Anna pulled back her hair and pinned it against the back of her head and then slipped on the glasses that Alastair had just given her.

Alastair was always developing new gear and Anna often was the initial recipient of his new and cutting-edge equipment. Alastair trusted her opinion and knew that she wouldn't divulge the knowledge of any of his secret devices to possible competitors. The glasses were designed to counteract the scan of facial recognition software by redirecting the angle and position of the wearer's iris. Miniscule beams ran across the frames, projecting the incorrect position of facial features back to the scanning computer. Alastair could also upload an alias that would be related to false recognition. Each time a positive facial recognition was made it was attributed to a false identity.

Anna slipped on the black rectangular frames and grabbed the garment bag from the corner of the bed and walked out to reveal the look to Alastair and Simon.

"What do you think?" Anna held her arms out and gave her best basic smile. The kind that she learned wouldn't draw any attention or stand out in anyone's memory.

"Perfectly plain, just how you want it," Simon said.

"Sit in line with my camera and we will set up your alias for the facial recognition," Alastair nodded toward a chair he placed in front of his computer and had already aligned with Anna's height.

Within a few seconds of Anna sitting down, Alastair began to work away behind his computer. His rapid keystrokes the only sound revealing his work behind the screen.

"There. You are now Jane Shelley from Virginia. Dressmaker and divorcee," Alastair looked pleased as he smiled at Anna. "You officially are a plain Jane."

"Nice," Anna was impressed with the swiftness that Alastair could alter a computer scan, and have it uploaded and in government systems. She often reminded herself that she was glad he was on her side.

Simon handed Anna the keys to the van he had parked in front of the building, complete with the clean license plate he attached while she was changing earlier.

Anna thanked both Simon and Alastair and made her way out of the building and into the van without being seen by anyone who could recognize her. Anna rehearsed the name and life that Alastair had created for her. She took a circuitous route to approach from the opposite end of town knowing she and her vehicle would be captured by traffic cameras set up around the White House. She wanted all roads to be pointing away from her.

Anna followed the instructions and approached the entrance that was reserved for staff and caterers for the state dinner. She was directed to visitor parking once her identification credentials were approved, and she was given a temporary badge to wear while she was in the building.

Anna knew from previous operations that the badge had a tiny tracking chip embedded between the layers of paper. Every step was monitored and recorded by security.

Anna pulled the van beside a compact blue Honda civic and put the vehicle in park. She was leery of approaching Eloria. Even with everything that Denis had done, he was her partner and she still cared for him. She also found with each layer of information that was peeled away from Denis's story, she could understand why he could have been driven to do what he did. Not that she agreed with his methods, however, when she tried, she couldn't imagine how she would've reacted if her father was betrayed and their family was torn apart the way Denis's was.

Anna pulled on the side door handle and pulled it toward her body and it slid along the metal track smoothly until it was open all the way. Simon had staged the interior of the van to look like a mobile seamstress' office knowing that security would more than likely look inside as all guests were instructed to leave their cars unlocked while parked on the property. Anna wanted to make sure that the two guards standing in the lot had a clear view of the contents inside the van, and removed the garment bag slowly.

Anna closed the van door and turned to walk toward the security entrance she was instructed to enter through. The security detail inside the door scanned her visitor's pass and entered the information from the false identification cards Alastair had created for her. As she waited the guard glanced at his computer screen and watched as the facial recognition system returned a clear confirmation of Jane Shelley. A divorced seamstress from Virginia.

Anna was guided down the long hallway and there she was met with a frazzled looking assistant who stood tapping her foot completely unaware the clip on the left side of her hair was drooping and the corner of her blouse was untucked from her pant waist.

Anna approached her with a blank expression, "I have the dress and the alterations requested. Can you direct me please?"

"I am supposed to take you there," the young assistant stammered. "You wouldn't believe how crazy things are here today!" The assistant walked quickly and after the first couple of steps it was clear she was wearing shoes she picked for looks and not comfort. Her short, quick steps mirrored her speaking pattern as she scurried ahead of Anna toward the room that Eloria would be for her final fitting.

Anna was thankful when they reached the room, if not for her eagerness to finally meet Eloria, but for her desire to give the frazzled assistant one less thing to worry about today. She wished Anna well and was off in a flash, striking one item off the list that was attached to her clipboard, and she could hear the assistant's phone buzz as she closed the door behind her.

Anna looked around the room and was impressed by the simplicity of the interior decoration. The paint on the wall was a soft, muted, historical color of yellow. The furniture was sparse and looked to have been chosen for comfort and long conversation and not as ornamental pieces. The art that hung on the walls was comprised of vintage charcoal sketches of old European towns. Each frame was made of slim strips of mahogany-colored wood and equally spaced. Anna wondered if Eloria had decorated the room herself. It seemed a more personal and private space than an official meeting room.

Anna walked with a slow smooth step as she took in each scene hanging on the wall in front of her. She stopped when she reached one that resembled the home that she was presumably raised in with her brothers and parents. The same one that she and Simon had just stood in front of a few days earlier. Underneath was penciled one word. Mājas. Anna knew it meant 'home' in Latvian. She thought back to reading Eloria's bio and remembered that she was a good artist, among other things.

Anna was now standing near her personal writing desk which was placed in front of a window that looked out onto the lawn and took in the magnificent gardens below. Anna wondered if Eloria placed the sketch of her childhood home near the window as a reminder of the stark contrast of her life from then to now, or if it was just a coincidence. Anna glanced at her watch and saw she had ten minutes until she was scheduled to meet Eloria. She took the time to look through her desk knowing that if there was anything there that could give her a clue as to what Eloria and her brothers were doing, it would be hidden quite well.

Anna felt under the edge of the desk and along the legs for a button or depression that may release a secret door with no luck. She pulled open the top drawer and moved the pads of paper, photos of Eloria with dignitaries, and loose pens around and pulled at the bottom of the drawer to see if it revealed a secret layer. As she cautiously looked through the drawer her eye caught sight of a vintage rectangular brass box that sat on a shelf on the bookshelf in the corner. Anna closed the drawer and walked toward the bookshelf and the vintage container.

It had caught Anna's eye because Denis had an identical one that sat on the corner of his desk in his office. Anna remembered back to one time when she had admired the box with its intricate design impressed into the antique metal and asked Denis where he found such a beautiful box. He had said that he received it from a relative when he graduated.

Anna slowly lifted the lid to the box and when she looked inside, she saw a collection of old jewelry pieces and decorative broaches inside. She never looked inside the box on Denis's desk, choosing to respect his privacy, however, she was sure his box did not contain the same items. Anna moved the pieces around and realized the inside of the box looked smaller than what the outside would have indicated. She took the tip of her nail and pulled back the red velvet base and leaned forward as it began to lift.

As the jeweled items slid to one side, the hidden base revealed two sole contents. A jump drive and a vial that was identical to the one Dr. Petrov had sold to Logan just moments before he was killed.

Anna wondered how Eloria came to have the vial but then remembered that it was Denis who retrieved the vial from Logan just after he killed him in the cemetery. Now Anna was certain that Eloria and Denis were in contact with each other and were most definitely working on the same secret operation together.

Anna quickly removed the vial and jump drive and slipped them into her pant pocket and then replaced the velvet base of the box and moved the jewelry around to cover the bottom evenly. She closed the lid and lowered the latch and then moved to stand near the chair that she folded the garment bag on.

Within a few minutes, and precisely on time Eloria, or the First Lady, arrived for her scheduled refitting.

She entered the room and Anna was struck by the similarity she held to Denis. It wasn't just her physical features. She was tall, had broad cheekbones, and low angled brown eyes just like Denis did, but with the added feminine beauty that obviously set her apart from every other woman, she would have been around. It was more about the way she carried herself. She spent so much time with Denis that the likeness jumped out at Anna even before the physical similarities did.

She strode with smoothness and confidence and walked up to Anna with her hand extended greeting her with all the warmth and familiarity of an old friend.

"I hope I didn't keep you waiting," Eloria apologized. "I see it's not just my office that has assistants filling in on this busy day," Eloria said about Anna's presence as well as her frazzled assistant's state.

"No," Anna replied. "I am not the regular seamstress."

"I was surprised to hear there needed to be an alteration. I was with Olga last week, and as usual, she had everything ready to go. Let's look then, shall we?" Eloria made her way toward the garment bag and pulled the zipper down and when she pulled open the vinyl cover revealing the pink satin atrocity inside, she turned to Anna with a laugh and said, "There must be some mistake."

Anna thought to a bridesmaid being forced to wear the dress and said, "You're not kidding."

"I'm sorry, I'm a bit confused," Eloria crossed her arms in front of her body waiting for an explanation from Anna.

"Your dress is arriving later today as initially scheduled. I'm here for a different reason," Anna's furtive tone was met with a more serious expression from Eloria.

"And that would be?" Eloria asked.

"I am here because of Blackwater," Anna said. "And your brother, Denis."

CHAPTER 30-

Eloria stood unresponsively and if it were not for a minuscule movement in her cheek, Anna would have thought she made a miscalculated judgment in Eloria's connection to Denis. For a few seconds, the two stood staring at each other, neither attempting to break the silence that filled the space between them. Anna waited for Eloria to show a sign or for her to make a move of some sort. Instead, she slowly placed the garment bag over the back of a red chair in the corner and walked over to her desk.

She began to sit and busy herself with her datebook, "I think you have made a terrible mistake. You should leave now before I contact security."

Anna didn't have the time nor the interest to play around to get Eloria to admit that she was Denis's sister. Time was not on Anna's side and neither was their location. She had to act carefully. Anna pulled the vial out of her pant pocket as she walked up behind Eloria. She reached over her shoulder and placed the vial of amber liquid on the desk, next to Eloria's datebook.

"What is that?" Eloria said without turning to face Anna.

"You know exactly what that is. It is the vial that Dr. Petrov sold to Logan James in Riga. Denis stole it from him just after he attacked us both and killed Logan to get it," Anna revealed.

"I don't know what you are talking about," Eloria said.

"I don't know exactly what you and Denis are up to Eloria, and to tell you the truth I think I am even a little sympathetic to what you have been through. However, people have died because of whatever you and your brothers have started, and it needs to stop. Nothing you do is going to change your past," Anna suddenly stepped back as Eloria swung her body around on her chair, grabbing the vial as she stood.

"Don't you tell me that nothing is going to change! Sure, it won't bring our parents back or replace the loss of Oskar, but it will let us right some wrongs," Eloria looked Anna directly in the eye and she could see the hurt and pain.

"A lot of innocent people have died Eloria. People I care about," Anna said.

"And more innocent people are going to lose their lives. But not because of what we're doing. We're trying to stop it from happening," Eloria explained.

"What are you talking about?" Anna asked.

"Denis was sent away and Oskar and I were left to deal with the destruction left by the Russians. You have no idea what they did to us," Eloria shook her head, "You don't even have any idea what's happening. You were raised in complete protection from such things."

"Over the last few days, I have been trying to understand how difficult it must have been for the three of you. And I'm sure I can only scratching the surface of the hurt. I don't know what exactly you had to go through, but I'm trying because it may help me to understand what caused Denis to do what he did. I need to make sense of it," Anna explained.

"We did what we had to. There was a monster created when Quantum could expand their business from just security to transportation. They found a way to take over ownership of many smaller companies. Utilities mostly. To control the power grid so they could control certain industries from a backdoor approach. I spent some time as an agent for Quantum and learned how their system worked. I stayed long enough to learn what was going on and then we realized we had an obligation to make things right."

"Like targeting Boris Ivanov?" Anna said, "I think you are going to use that vial to do it." Anna recognized the same sense of conviction in Eloria's voice that she so often saw in Denis.

Eloria laughed, "You think I am going to kill Ivanov? You have no idea of how much is happening right under your nose? Ivanov is just a pawn, a small and insignificant monster."

"Let the UN deal with him. Bring all the information to them and they will punish him the way he should be punished, on the world stage." Anna pleaded.

"Ivanov deserves to be punished greatly for what he did to our family. He tortured and abused many innocent people in our village just because we tried to stand up to the Russians for our freedom. And then the Americans reneged on their promise to get us out of Riga. My parents died because of what they both did to us. He deserves to be strung up, that is what he deserves." Eloria paused and shook her head. "But now we need to use him so no one else suffers the way we did, and although his punishment will not be as great as it should be, it'll have to suffice."

"What plan? What are you talking about?" Anna asked.

"I told you that you have no idea how big this is. Governments have been playing these games since the beginning of time. Power makes the government forget their people, their purpose. And the lure of more power and control can turn the most honest of world leaders into monsters like Ivanov." Eloria said.

"I don't believe that," Anna said.

Eloria let out a restrained laugh, intended to mock Anna's sentiment, "Denis told me you were an idealistic agent. He said he found it charming and refreshing."

Anna tensed at the mention of Denis's name. She was still torn between caring about him as her partner and friend and feeling that he had betrayed her. "I became an agent to defend the principles of democracy, not to mock them."

Eloria crossed her arms in front of her chest and leaned against the wall behind her. "You probably think that your government would not allow such things to happen now? But you would be very wrong Anna."

"I know there are corrupt people in the government, but there is no way that a democracy like ours would allow countries and innocent families to be taken advantage of.

That's not what we stand for," Anna was passionate about the strength and importance of a democratic government, and she was willing to die to defend it. Just as her father did.

"Do you think Ashbury was the only one in control at Quantum? Do you think that all decisions stopped with him? Have you noticed any outcry or collapse of Quantum or any of its subsidiaries upon his death?" Eloria fired the questions at Anna, not intending on waiting for a response.

Anna had been surprised how quiet the news was about Quantum, she just chalked it up to an attempt to keep the public calm. "If you know that there are other people in the government that are part of Quantum then come forward with their names and let the courts deal with them!"

"The corruption goes further than you know Anna," Eloria said, "There is no way to stop it. Courts, Government, it's everywhere."

"How about your husband? He is the President. Surely, he would believe you. He could make sure the right people pay."

"He is the last person who would help," Eloria said. "There is only one way we can try to make things right."

Anna caught how Eloria emphasized the word *last* and let the realization sink in before she responded, "Do you mean the President is involved?"

Eloria slowly nodded as Anna realized the unfortunate reality of the situation, "You see, I cannot go to my husband, because he is one of the few left in control of how Quantum uses its power. If innocent people weren't going to be hurt, you could admire its brilliance in the simplicity of their setup. They control companies from the inside, making decisions that affect the social and economic fabric of the country, and then they swoop in and reap the spoils. The hero that controls the events that lead to its praise."

Anna was dumbfounded and couldn't speak.

"Right now, as we speak, my husband is planning to use the connections with Quantum to cut off essential services to people in Venezuela. In a very short while companies will have to lay off staff, people will feel the sting of the economic loss, they will rebel and cause social unrest. Crime will rise and the government will have no choice but to reach out to stronger democratic countries for help. In comes the President with an offer of support and as an act of desperation Venezuela will allow the U.S.-owned companies to come in and help rebuild the country. They'll be able to make money from their natural resources and will look like saviors doing it."

"You are telling me the President knows about Quantum?" Anna said.

"Knows about it?! They are responsible for him becoming President in the first place," Eloria said. "It's not just foreign companies they're controlling."

"Do you have proof? I mean solid proof?" Anna asked.

"Yes, it is all on a jump drive. I am assuming you also found it since it was with the vial in the box," Eloria said. "How did you find it?"

"Denis had the same box on his desk, and I thought it was too much of a coincidence. So, I took a chance," Anna explained. Eloria nodded her head.

"Let me take the evidence to the right people. We can uncover this together," Anna pleaded.

"No. They'll be able to stop any of this from getting out. There is only one way to stop any more of this from happening," Eloria said.

"What is that?" Anna asked.

Eloria held Dr. Petrov's vial in her closed fist, "I'm going to administer this to the President and Ivanov is going to be framed for it. Several documents will connect Ivanov to the control of Quantum as well as the plans for Venezuela."

"Why?" Anna asked.

"The world will be more likely to take action if they believe there's Russian interference over democratic countries. Especially if he has recently killed the U.S. President at a state function," Eloria explained.

And before Anna could protest any further, she felt the cold metal of a pipe as it made contact on the back of her head with the full force that only came from an intentional attack. Anna's head began to swirl, and a feeling of nausea rose in her gut as she crumpled into a heap onto the floor. And as each breath became shallower, the room went dark.

CHAPTER 31-

Anna rose unsteadily to her feet. The throbbing from where she was struck, wrapped around the sides of her head and gave her a painful crushing sensation. Instinctively, Anna drew her hands up and grabbed the sides of her head, the pain was excruciating, and her disorientation was only complicated by the lack of light in the room.

Anna stumbled forward with small calculated steps with her right arm outstretched in the blacked room until she was able to locate the edge of a wall, or more hopefully, a door.

After five steps Anna was stopped by the feeling of cold stone on the palm of her hand. She placed her other hand on the wall and realized she was no longer in Eloria's private room. Anna cursed herself for not being more aware of what was going on around her. Then an odd thought crossed her mind. Was it Denis that struck her on the head? The thought sent a chill up her spine as she realized he had attacked her twice in the last month, almost leaving her for dead.

Anna patted her way along the wall moving to her left and came to a stop when she felt the trim of a door frame with her hand. She maneuvered her hand midway down the door frame until she felt the door handle. The steel handle was cold under her grip and when she tried to turn it, but it didn't move. She released her grip from the door and reached into the waistband of her pants and slipped a metal tripwire out from within the seam of her pant.

Anna inserted the tripwire into the lock and wiggled it around until the lock pins inside the lock released their hold. When Anna felt the click of the lock releasing, she slowly turned the handle and pulled the door open.

She was surprised to find she was looking at a work area for the grounds crew of the White House. She wasn't aware of how long she had been unconscious but the light in the sky put the time at late afternoon. Anna slipped out of the room and realized it was an outdoor shed used to house equipment for the lawn's keeper.

She made her way around the work crews and security guards and emerged at the far end of the parking lot where she was parked.

Anna walked quickly and determinedly toward the parked van and slipped into the driver's seat before she could be seen. She took advantage of the pre-dinner commotion and exited the grounds before Eloria, or her attacker would be aware of her escape. When she was safely clear of the area, she dialed Simon's cell phone number.

Simon picked up on the second ring, "Where have you been? Are you alright?" Simon frantically shouted into the phone.

"I'm on my way back," Anna responded, surprised at how pleased she was with Simon's concern.

"What happened? Did you find Eloria?"

"Yeah, I found her. You are not going to believe what they are planning," Anna spoke as she weaved around traffic hoping she chose the fastest route back to where Simon and Alastair were waiting.

"They?" Alastair was now speaking after Simon put the call on speaker.

"I was struck from behind while I was trying to convince Eloria to go public with her information. She was planning on something other than killing Ivanov. They planned to kill the President and frame Ivanov."

"Why would she kill her husband?" Simon asked.

"I don't think that theirs is a marriage of love. Anyways, there's more. She said something, that if it's true, is very disturbing. She claimed the President is part of Quantum, a huge part, and apparently, they planned an attack on Venezuela." Anna slammed on her brakes as the traffic light quickly turned from green to red, controlled by a security procession that cleared the intersection in front of her. Both Simon and Alastair were silent on the other end of the line.

"That confirms what we heard Boris Ivanov planning earlier today. He was meeting with some of his American counterparts to plan a covert entrance into Venezuela," Simon explained.

She watched as the procession of delegates from foreign countries passed in front of her. The intersection was lined with security police on motorcycles on both sides of the intersection and between them, limousines adorned with flags from various countries passed through the intersection. Anna caught sight of the Russian dignitary's car and watched as it passed through the intersection and on its way to the state dinner.

"What time is the dinner tonight?" Anna asked.

"It is slated to begin in about ninety minutes."

The security police left the intersection following the last limousine away from Anna's position. Anna depressed the accelerator pedal as the light turned green and she rushed the remainder of the distance to where she parked outside her building. Anna flung open the front door and burst into the room.

"Now what?" Alastair asked.

Anna walked straight to the kitchen and opened the cupboard with the ibuprofen. She popped the seal and tipped two pills into her hand and then after a pause, tipped out two more. She placed the bottle on the counter and then grabbed a glass and filled it with cold water from the dispenser on the fridge. After she swallowed the pills she returned to the next room and began to devise a plan with Simon and Alastair.

"I don't know how, but we have to get into the state dinner tonight. That may be the only way to keep Eloria from doing something regrettable." Simon said.

"Is it?" Anna asked as she tossed herself into the large reading chair at the far end of the room.

Alastair and Simon exchanged a shocked look with each other then stared at Anna waiting for her response.

"Well, think about it. How bad would it be to have one of the major heads of Quantum removed? And at the same time, Eloria is taking care of Ivanov, who should have been jailed long ago," Anna closed her eyes and tilted her head back.

Simon was the first to speak. "You know we can't let that happen, Anna. It's not why we signed on for this."

Anna knew Simon was right, but how were they going to uncover what Quantum was doing when it went this deep?

"How are we going to do it, Simon?" Anna felt lost. She had never been this deep in an operation without Denis or William to count on. She had to depend on Simon, who she had learned not to trust for so long.

"What would William always suggest when we found ourselves too deep into an operation when it got complicated?" Simon asked as if he knew Anna was thinking about him.

Anna allowed a small smile to cross her face, "He would say to take it back to basics."

"Exactly! And that is precisely what we'll do."

Alastair stood from his computer and pulled two cards from the side laminating and printing machine he had on the table. He handed Simon and Anna each a hotel identity card.

"Really think this could work again?" Anna said.

"Why not?" Simon smiled and raised his eyebrows, "But we will have to hurry, there isn't much time left."

Simon and Anna quickly got changed and left the apartment and headed in the direction of the hotel.

Alastair returned to his computer and shuddered as Denis's old tracking chip blinked to life.

CHAPTER 32-

Getting into the hotel was an easier proposition than Anna had thought. She and Simon had planned to split up to search for Eloria and Ivanov, which didn't take long. Eloria and Anna spotted each other simultaneously. Eloria turned and quickly walked away from the group she was speaking with and wove her way through the crowded room toward the far side of the floor. Anna could see she was headed for the exit and pushed her way through guests trying not to lose sight of her. Now and again a guest would ask for a refill, and Anna just ignored their request and kept moving in Eloria's direction. Her hastened exit caught the attention of her assistant who began to follow her toward the exit.

As Anna was figuring out how to derail the assistant, she saw Simon grab her arm and distracted her with an elaborate question about the service. It was just enough time for Anna to follow Eloria through the exit and down the back-service hall to where she saw the end of Eloria's gown as she entered a private room off to the left.

Anna burst through the door. "Eloria, don't do this! You are going to regret it. I can help you get your message heard," Anna pleaded with Eloria.

"It's too late anyway," Eloria had a determined look in her eye and Anna knew she was telling the truth. "I have already added the poison to Harris' drinks and placed the vial with some of the poison in Ivanov's hotel room," Eloria shook her head and smiled. "You see, all your best efforts have gone to waste. All the President's drinks are prepared by separate service personnel for security purposes. I made sure one of our operatives was placed inside and Harris will be served only drinks that have been laced with the poison. The President will be dead by dinner and Ivanov will be to blame."

"Eloria there has to be a better way," Anna began to try and dissuade Eloria and then noticed she pulled a small vial out of her handbag and popped the top of the lid and began to lift it to her mouth.

"Wait!" Anna shouted. At that moment, the First Lady's assistant entered the room just as Eloria had lifted the liquid to her mouth.

"What is going on?" the assistant yelled. Even though she did not know what was happening, she instinctively knew the First Lady was in danger.

"Help me stop her!" Anna shouted at the assistant just as Eloria tossed back the liquid. Anna and the assistant both ran toward Eloria and caught her as she began to fall back onto the ground. Anna turned to the assistant and yelled at her to go and get help.

The assistant ran out of the room without questioning who Anna was or what the First Lady was doing.

"Eloria! Why?" Anna pleaded. "After everything you have been through. Why not keep fighting?"

"I have done what I came to do, I can go no further. It is up to the others now," Eloria gave Anna a warm smile as her eyes faded. "Denis always said you and I would have gotten along well. I can see it too. I know why he cared for you."

Anna held Eloria as her body gave in to the poison and went limp.

CHAPTER 33-

Anna was halfway down the hall and back inside the crowded ballroom when she heard the medical team rush into the room where Eloria lay dead. Simon was on the other side of the room making his way to where Ivanov stood next to a potted fern, deep in conversation with the delegate from Britain.

The server who had carried the President his previous drink was passing by where Anna stood, and she noticed the gin and tonic perched in the center of the tray with the Presidential seal emblazoned on it. Anna grabbed the tray from the young server.

"Joseph wants to see you NOW!" Anna said.

"Who?" the server was confused.

"Our supervisor! He is super pissed with you," Anna took the tray and began to walk toward the President leaving the young server perplexed as to who Joseph was or what she did to displease him.

Anna walked up to President Sanderson who was momentarily alone and held the tray close to her body. He nodded and began to reach for the glass that stood in the center of the tray.

"I don't think this drink is to your liking sir," Anna spoke in a low but assertive tone.

"Excuse me?" The President said with a confused tone.

"I am wondering how long you thought that your involvement with Quantum could stay silent?" Anna asked with a straight face. She knew she probably didn't have much time knowing that the First Lady was lying dead in a room down the hall.

"Are you a reporter?" the President made a motion with his raised hand toward the security detail that was standing a few feet behind them.

"I wouldn't do that sir, after all, your wife has given me all the information I need to prove you are deeply involved in Quantum." President Sanderson lowered his arm after waving off the guard and with a low voice leaned in toward Anna, "Maybe we should speak in the next room?"

Anna followed President Sanderson into a private room behind the ballroom. Once they were both securely inside, he turned to Anna and crossed his arms over his chest.

"What do you exactly think you are doing here? This is a state dinner, and we don't have time for nosy reporters looking to stir up trouble."

"If you really thought that sir, you would have had me removed in the ballroom."

"I just didn't want to make a scene."

"Are you sure it wasn't about the information that your wife gave me?" Anna asked.

"You're bluffing," President Sanderson said.

"Let's get one thing clear. I'm not a reporter and I'm one of the few remaining members of an elite investigative division the government had set up. One that Ashbury had tried to decommission by planting an explosive in our building. You may remember that explosion a couple of years back?"

"I still don't know what you are talking about," the President said.

"As much as I despise you right now, I am trying to save your life. This drink has been poisoned on the direction and instruction of your wife." Anna said.

The look of shock came across President Sanderson's face too quickly for him to hide.

"Eloria, or Mary as you know her, is part of a rebel sect from Latvia. It goes much deeper than you, but she uncovered your involvement in Quantum and what you are planning in Venezuela and she had planned to stop you."

Anna lifted the tray slightly, "She had this drink poisoned knowing you would be consuming it before dinner, and she planted the remaining poison in Ivanov's room to frame him."

"Why Ivanov?" President Sanderson's question proved to Anna that he believed what she was saying.

"He is responsible for her parent's death and the separation of her family. He was never held accountable for his crimes in Latvia and she saw it as an easy way to kill two birds with one stone. If you will pardon the pun."

President Sanderson crossed his arms in front of his chest and raised his chin and continued to fain his best attempt at a poker face.

"I don't know what game you are playing at, but I think this has gone far enough," President Sanderson began to reach for the phone on his desk when Anna pulled out the jump drive that she had tucked into her sleeve.

"It's all here. The Latvian cover-up, the divisions of Quantum, and their involvement in rogue countries, and there's even a section on your path to this office. Voter tampering, bribery, and your connection to Quantum."

"Why don't we have Mary explain this?" President Sanderson asked.

"We can't," Anna said.

"Why not?"

The door to the private room swung open and a frantic Secret Service agent entered the room.

"Yes, what is it?" Sanderson snapped.

"It's the First Lady, Mr. President," the agent stammered. "She's dead."

CHAPTER 34-

Once the agent had alerted the President to the First Lady's demise, a team of twelve personnel had amassed in the room waiting for instructions from the President on how to proceed.

The President held his hand to his forehead and the team stood to wait in silence as he thought.

He lowered his hand and pushed his shoulders back, "No word of this tonight." He looked toward the press secretary's shocked face. "Put out an announcement that the First Lady will regrettably not be joining us as she is feeling ill."

He then motioned toward Anna, "This young server has alerted me that this drink has been tampered with by one of Ivanov's men. Please have it tested and Ivanov's room searched. Then, and only if, you find evidence of any poison are you to take him into custody. Otherwise, this could be a diplomatic mess."

The President's staff jumped into action, and before Anna could protest the glass and tray were whisked out of Anna's hand and she was led from the room. Sanderson pulled her in close to his body appearing to thank her but whispered in her ear to hand over the evidence that Eloria gave her or suffer the same fate as she did. Anna reluctantly slipped the jump drive into the palm of his hand as he stared coldly back into her eyes.

The President was then escorted out of the room surrounded by three Secret Service bodyguards, the press secretary was dictating a response to her assistant, and Anna was left with two Secret Service guards who were instructing her not to mention a word of what happened this evening to anyone.

And as they took down the information from her false security badge, she stood in disbelief.

The Secret Service agents took ten minutes to interrogate and instruct Anna on what she was permitted, and not permitted, to say. She knew what they were going to say before they even opened their mouths. Anna just listened, nodded, and waited patiently through the process until she could leave.

When she entered back into the main ballroom, she found Simon and gave him the predetermined signal that it was time to leave.

Anna filled Simon in on the evening's events as they drove away from the hotel.

"I can't believe you gave him the jump drive!"

"I said I gave him a jump drive, not the jump drive," Anna smirked.

Simon glanced at Anna as he was driving, "What exactly did you give him?"

"It was a copy of the jump drive, but with an added feature," Anna explained.

"Is that what you and Alastair were doing just before we left?"

Anna nodded, "I had him install a trigger feature. Once any files are opened, an automatic email feature is enabled, and the contents of the entire drive will be sent to every news agency in the country. That way, the documents are coming from the White House directly and there will be little reason to double-check the facts."

"Now all we need to do is wait for President Sanderson to check the jump drive," Simon said.

"And then wait for the fallout," Anna looked out the window of the car as they passed under the lights on the Arlington Bridge and wondered if Denis would blame her for Eloria's death.

CHAPTER 35-

Ivanov left the state dinner with his security detail secure with the belief that he and Sanderson had finalized their plan to begin to secure the resources in Venezuela over the next ten months.

Ivanov had spent many years involved with government, and some moments held memories that he would soon rather forget. He worked tirelessly after being acquitted in his trial twenty-five years ago, to ensure the generation that followed him would not commit the same war crimes he had been involved in himself. He had failed miserably where his own son was concerned.

He spent more time in his diplomatic position bailing his son out of trouble only to have him throw his past in his face.

"It's still not as bad as what you have done," he would scream in response to his father's reprisals.

Ivanov eventually fell back into the role of a man with slack morals and little concern for the weaker or the oppressed. He grew a little thicker and balder with age, but the real change was deep inside. He grew harder and even he didn't think that was possible. His attitude toward his son was of distrust and disdain and his will was altered, leaving everything to the daughter he fathered with his mistress two years after Mikhail was born. He would often chuckle that his only regret was that he wouldn't be alive to see his face when the will was read.

One of Ivanov's guards held his elbow as he lowered himself into the waiting limousine. His guards knew to shield their boss' body whenever they assisted his movements. Ivanov grew large and his labored breathing was obvious to everyone but himself. The limousine rocked slightly with the addition of his weight in the back seat and once his legs were securely inside, the guard closed the door and the limousine began the drive back to Ivanov's hotel.

Upon arrival, Ivanov had expected Mikhail to be waiting in the front lobby for an update of the evening meeting with President Sanderson. Ivanov grunted when he viewed the empty lobby as he entered behind his lead guard.

"Take me to Mikhail's room," Ivanov snapped at his guard who then pressed the elevator button that would deliver them to the floor Mikhail was staying on.

Ivanov walked with a harsh step and each time he lowered his foot it reverberated through the empty hall as they approached Mikhail's room.

"Open it," Ivanov shouted ahead to the guard standing outside Mikhail's room. And without taking a pause in his step, he entered the room and then came to a full stop at the foot of Mikhail's bed.

There lay Mikhail. Waxy with the complexion that only death can render, along with a needle protruding from his left arm that lay outstretched beside him. Ivanov looked down at his son and felt no sadness, only regret that he may have failed his son in the end.

He instructed his guards to clean up the evidence and to call the Russian embassy officials to take care of the necessary paperwork. Ivanov turned and walked out of the room and directly down the hall toward the elevator. Ivanov noticed a hotel room service clerk walking ahead of them and called out.

"You, server. Wait!" Ivanov's booming voice rarely gave cause for him to repeat any instructions he hurled at staff.

The server stopped and turned to face Ivanov and the two guards that were walking toward him. Ivanov pulled two one-hundred-dollar bills from his pocket and slapped them in the server's hand.

"Bring a bottle of Lagavulin to the suite on the tenth floor," Ivanov instructed and without waiting for an acknowledgment from the server he walked around him and to the waiting elevator where he disappeared behind the embossed brass doors.

Denis then slipped the bills into his pocket and made his way down the stairwell and out to his waiting car in the back alley.

CHAPTER 36-

Morning came sooner than Anna had desired and the throbbing in her head persisted even though a couple of days had passed since she was attacked in Eloria's room. She forced herself up to a sitting position on the edge of the bed and tipped a couple of pills into the palm of her hand and chased them back with the glass of water sitting on her night table. Anna had returned home and had forced herself to take a much-needed break and rest. Anna's body ached as she made her way into the bathroom and showered. She processed the previous day's events and even though she knew that what Eloria had planned was wrong, she regretted not being able to help her in the end, and she came to see her in a more positive light than when she began. Then her thoughts naturally moved to Denis and she wondered how he took the death of his sister.

Denis and Anna now had the painful similarity in their lives that they were alone and without family. She realized that maybe that was all they left had in common.

Forty-eight hours had passed since the state dinner and the news channels and daily papers were alive with breaking news that was constantly being splashed across the pages and screens. Every couple of hours saw a new headline and new shocking revelation being brought to light. The turmoil and upset contradicted a relatively peaceful administration that held the promise of economic growth and expanded health care.

Initially, the country was glued to the continuous flow of news with the announcement of the First Lady's death due to complications from an appendicitis attack. As the country grieved the loss of such a young, vibrant woman, the President saw his popularity numbers soar. Before Eloria's death, Sanderson's numbers were perpetually dropping. However, with the overwhelming sadness that the country was feeling at the loss of their First Lady, it seemed as if sympathy was a motivating factor in the support the country was willing to put behind their newly widowed President.

President Sanderson rode the wave of popularity as his administration announced the trade deal that was signed with a few economically strong countries and Venezuela to work together to build a refugee program to help those hurt by war and failed trade deals. It included plans of large American conglomerates moving into the once restrictive Venezuelan marketplace and helping to revitalize growth.

Anna became angry and disheartened at the thought that people like William and her father died for nothing if it was to protect the freedom and protection of corrupt men like Sanderson.

Her despair was not to last long as Anna glanced at the most recent morning headlines that crawled across the ticker tape at the base of the news screen. Finally. Sanderson had triggered the release of all the information that she, Simon, and Alastair had uncovered. Photos of the documents proving Quantum's involvement in illicit trade and corporate take over, Sanderson's scripted rise to office, and even how Sonja innocently uncovered information and then died the night she mailed it to Josh. Everything was there for not only the country but the world to see.

The news also finally covered the mysterious deaths of both Boris and Mikhail Ivanov, who passed away on the same evening. However, because of diplomatic immunity, both of their bodies were whisked back to Russia where they were to handle all the formal details of any investigation.

Anna muted the television and sat in the overstuffed reading chair by the window and thought back to the previous evening dinner with Alastair and Simon. Alastair was booked on a return flight to England and Simon's services have been engaged for a covert operation in Kazakhstan. Simon had tried most of the evening to convince Anna to join him, but she flatly refused.

After the emotionally draining year she had, she felt she needed to take time off. Maybe she would go to Banff, where she could recharge in the surrounding mountains and fresh air. Her father would take her and her mother there every year for a vacation.

When the three were saying goodbye to each other and preparing to get into their separate taxis, Simon slipped an airline ticket to Kazakhstan into her pocket and told her if she changed her mind, he could really use her. He then kissed her on the cheek and climbed into his waiting taxi and was gone.

Anna was remembering the feeling of Simon's kiss when she was startled by a knock. She shuffled her body toward the door and pulled it open.

"Denis!" Anna was standing face to face with her old partner, once thought dead, and now more like a stranger.

Denis smiled and walked past Anna who stood shocked and amazed that after all this time she was within arm's reach of him. Denis walked into the apartment and took a seat in front of the muted television with news blasts that flashed across the screen. "A lot has happened since we last saw each other." Denis looked soft and worn, and for a moment, Anna felt sorry for him.

"I'm sorry you got caught up in everything. We had our plan in motion by the time we met. It just didn't seem like a good idea to get you involved," Denis explained.

"You were probably right not to tell me," Anna's soft demeanor surprised even her.

"I'm glad you know the truth now. You're an important part of my life, Anna. You always will be," Anna wasn't sure, but she thought she saw tears forming along the rim of Denis's eyes.

"I'm sorry I couldn't stop Eloria from killing herself," Anna said.

Denis shook his head, "It's not your fault. Besides, she was so determined to make things right. To at least try and right some wrongs," Denis paused for a moment. "I'm glad you had a chance to meet her."

"So am I," Anna said.

The two sat silently just letting the peaceful moment last for as long as they could.

"Was that you that knocked me out at Eloria's?" Anna asked.

"Yeah, sorry," Denis said. "And sorry about the attack in the cemetery. I just wanted to stop you, not hurt you."

Anna nodded. She knew that if he wanted her dead, he would have done it in Riga. That had to count for something.

"Oh, I have something of yours," Anna jumped and walked over to her desk on the other side of the room. She pulled open the top drawer and pulled out the weathered photo she had carried with her since she left the safehouse in Latvia. Anna handed Denis the photo of him, Eloria, and Oskar when they were just children in their family village. Denis cradled the photo in his shaking hands and a tear rolled down his cheek. Anna felt a pang of sadness knowing after all they had been through that Denis was alone once again.

Denis wiped the tear from his cheek with the back of his right hand, "I have something for you as well." Denis pulled a small weathered brown leather journal from his jacket pocket and handed it to Anna. She recognized it immediately as her father's journal. "It explains a bit more about what kind of man your father was," Denis said as he released it to Anna's hands. "He was a good man Anna and you should know everything he did. I owe my life to him."

Anna ran her hand over the textured cover that her father's hands would have touched so many times before. She was eager to open it, but she wanted to be alone when she began to read his elegant handwriting and possibly be faced to deal with new secrets.

Denis slapped his hand on his knee and stood up from the chair, "I have to go know Anna. You will want to read that in private anyhow."

Anna wrapped her arms around Denis and he instantly returned the embrace. "We've both lost so much Anna, but there is still a lot of good left in us yet!" Denis leaned down and kissed Anna on her cheek. The opposite cheek where Simon left his kiss the night before.

Anna stood motionless as Denis walked toward the door. When he began to turn the handle she said, "When am I going to see you again?"

"Not sure, I have some business to take care of over the next few months. Maybe I will contact you then and we can start to reconnect and heal."

"That would be nice," Anna said.

Denis stepped into the hall and just before he closed the door Anna asked, "Where are you going?"

"Kazakhstan," Denis smiled, then closed the door.

Anna glanced at the time on the clock and decided she better pack quickly if she was going to make the flight.

THE END

Author's Note

Thank you for reading, and I sincerely hope you enjoyed *The Blackwater Operative,* the first in the Anna Ledin Spy Thriller Series. Please check out the other books by this author.

For a chance to win a free book, please visit:
www.llabbott.com/book-giveaway

Every month there's a new contest and every name on my email list is entered to win. Over and over and over again. Plus, you'll be the first to know about new releases or sales. Your personal information will never be divulged, shared, or sold. If you're on social media. . . I would love to have you follow along.

Thanks again, my best to you and yours.
L.L. Abbott

Books by L.L. Abbott

Mystery & Suspense

Thrillers

Teen & Young Adult

General Fiction